A lightning bolt of hunger shot through him.

This was supposed to be his game. His pursuit. She wasn't supposed to arouse him with a single touch. He was in charge of the seduction, of enticing her into surrendering her secrets.

Yet Ethan found himself threading his finger into Sienna's luxuriant waves and savoring the silky slide of the soft strands against his skin. He half closed his eyes and watched her expression transform from bold curiosity to wary anticipation. Which emotion would rule the day?

He had a plan to find out.

"Thanks for the fun night." Her soft breath puffed against his cheek before she kissed him and left him aching for more.

Worse, he no longer knew if she was playing him or if her sweetness was honest and legitimate. He searched her eyes for the flicker he'd seen over dinner, the one that matched the fire inside him.

And he found it.

* * *

Seduction, Southern Style by Cat Schield is part of the Sweet Tea and Scandal series.

Dear Reader,

I'm so excited to be journeying back to Charleston for this fifth installment of my Sweet Tea and Scandal series. I know many of you have been eagerly awaiting the reveal of the Watts heiress, and I hope you won't be too disappointed that this story is focused on her sister, Sienna Burns. I needed to give Ethan a counterpart who both confounded his expectations and gave him a feeling of belonging. Their romance is one of my favorites. I love how Sienna doesn't realize she's looking for her perfect match until the chemistry between her and Ethan awakens her sensuality and her confidence.

I ventured beyond Charleston for this book and you will get a glimpse of Savannah, as well. These two cities are both so beautiful and the perfect backdrop for this fantastic couple's love story. I hope you enjoy *Seduction, Southern Style*.

Happy reading!

Cat Schield

CAT SCHIELD

SEDUCTION, SOUTHERN STYLE

HARLEQUIN®
DESIRE™

Recycling programs for this product may not exist in your area.

ISBN-13: 978-1-335-23290-8

Seduction, Southern Style

Copyright © 2021 by Catherine Schield

This edition published by arrangement with Harlequin Books S.A.

For questions and comments about the quality of this book, please contact us at CustomerService@Harlequin.com.

Harlequin Enterprises ULC
22 Adelaide St. West, 40th Floor
Toronto, Ontario M5H 4E3, Canada
www.Harlequin.com

Printed in U.S.A.

Cat Schield is an award-winning author of contemporary romances for Harlequin Desire. She likes her heroines spunky and her heroes swoonworthy. While her jet-setting characters live all over the globe, Cat makes her home in Minnesota with her daughter, two opinionated Burmese cats and a goofy Doberman. When she's not writing or walking dogs, she's searching for the perfect cocktail or traveling to visit friends and family. Contact her at www.catschield.com.

Books by Cat Schield

Harlequin Desire

Sweet Tea and Scandal

Upstairs Downstairs Baby
Substitute Seduction
Revenge with Benefits
Seductive Secrets
Seduction, Southern Style

Dynasties: Seven Sins

Untamed Passion

Visit her Author Profile page at Harlequin.com, or catschield.com, for more titles!

You can also find Cat Schield on Facebook, along with other Harlequin Desire authors, at Facebook.com/harlequindesireauthors!

To Ella and Bri,
who took over for a couple weeks last summer
so I could write and make my deadline.
It was so much fun getting to know you!
Best of luck with your future endeavors.

One

Sienna Burns experienced a familiar thrill as the town car, carrying her and her adopted sister, Teagan, coasted along the tree-lined avenue in downtown Charleston. As an independent art consultant, Sienna spent a great deal of time traveling and always loved the opportunity to visit a new city. And this one was breathtaking. Picket and iron fences hid lush gardens transected by hedge-lined brick walkways and dotted with palm trees and bountiful hydrangeas. The pastel buildings with overflowing window boxes imprinted her mind with explosions of vibrant colors.

"This is really beautiful," she said, as one terraced, columned mansion after another flew by.

When her sister didn't respond, Sienna shifted attention to Teagan and wasn't surprised to find her taking a selfie. Teagan knew better than to ask Sienna to join her in the picture. With her dark hair and life-long weight issues, Sienna had always felt like a plump, shabby shadow of her beautiful, trendy sister and actively avoided the limelight.

"You should try and get one of these gorgeous mansions in the background," Sienna suggested as the car stopped at an intersection. "I'll bet your followers would love that."

"Uh-huh," Teagan mumbled, pouting at the screen and showing no indication that she was paying attention to her sister.

"Why am I even here?" Exhaustion sparked Sienna's temper. She hadn't slept during her eight-hour flight from London to New York or at any point during the hectic three-hour turnaround before Teagan had dragged her aboard the private jet for their flight to Charleston. "You've been glued to your phone the entire trip."

As different as the two sisters were in appearance and temperament, one trait they shared was that they never stopped working. Teagan had spun her status as a social media influencer into several successful businesses and was constantly promoting her jewelry and accessories lines, as well as her concierge makeup service.

"I need my sister with me." Without looking up from her phone, Teagan reached over to grip Sienna's hand, the biting clamp revealing the tension hidden behind her unruffled expression. "You know I'm freaked out about meeting my birth mom's family."

Several months earlier Sienna had been shocked to

hear that Teagan had submitted her DNA to a genetic testing service and discovered she was related to a prominent family in Charleston, South Carolina. The full details of how baby Teagan had come to be available to be adopted by a wealthy couple on the Upper East Side of New York might forever remain a mystery, but from what Teagan had patched together from talking with her Charleston family, it seemed that her biological mother, Ava Watts, had headed to the Big Apple in the hopes of becoming a fashion model only to become pregnant and die tragically, leaving behind her infant daughter. Apparently, Ava had cut herself off so thoroughly from her family that they hadn't discovered her death or that she'd had a daughter until many years after the fact. By then, Teagan had been adopted and the sealed court records had prevented her family from locating her.

"You shouldn't be," Sienna said, sandwiching Teagan's hand between hers and offering the comfort her sister craved. "They've been looking for you since learning you existed. I'm sure they're over the moon to have found you at last."

"Of course, but what if they don't like me?"

It never ceased to amaze Sienna that her beautiful, talented sister suffered bouts of insecurity. "What's not to love?"

"You're the best sister." Teagan leaned her head on Sienna's shoulder and absorbed all the support. "I don't know what I'd do without you."

Sienna's heart gave a painful wrench. "Luckily, you'll never have to find out."

Filled to the brim with optimism once more, Teagan turned back to her phone. Sienna released her sister's hand and returned her attention to the scenery they were passing, letting her delight in the charming view recharge the energy she'd poured into the other woman.

"You know it still amazes me how much I look like them." Teagan displayed the Instagram page belonging to her Charleston cousin, Dallas Shaw.

The image on the screen showed a smiling trio of blonde women. The twin cousins and their mother, Ava Watts's older sister, Lenora Shaw, bore an uncanny resemblance to Teagan. Sienna felt a tinge of jealousy as she imagined future pictures with her sister grinning alongside the trio, her long blond hair and riveting green eyes proof that she belonged to the Watts/Shaw clan.

"Even without the DNA test, there's little question you're related," Sienna said, overcome by a sudden blast of panic and misery at the thought of losing her sister to her new family.

"I hope they feel the same way."

"Of course they will," Sienna assured her, pushing aside her own anxiety and grief to bolster Teagan.

"I really wish you'd stay longer than a few days," Teagan said, continuing to scroll through her cousin's Instagram feed, skipping over the photos of beautifully plated dishes to focus on the images of Dallas and her identical sister, Poppy.

"This is your moment with your long-lost family," Sienna reminded her. "I don't want to overstay my welcome."

"Don't be silly. They're thrilled that you're coming with me. And... I told them you'd be here a couple weeks."

"What?" Sienna gasped, appalled. "Even if I could take that much time off, you don't know these people well enough to take advantage of their hospitality on my behalf."

"Are you kidding? You've barely taken any time off in the last three years so you're due for a vacation. And there's plenty of room at the estate. In fact, both Dallas and Poppy live on-site in the old caretaker's house. My aunt Lenora said there's an empty carriage house and bedrooms galore in the main house. Believe me, there's plenty of room."

"I'll rearrange some things and try to stay for a week."

"Ten days."

"I only packed enough for four." Yet even as she protested, her exhaustion worked against her. The idea of lingering in this charming city and behaving like a tourist was vastly appealing. The frenetic pace of her career kept her running on sheer adrenaline most of the time. What fun to just be lazy for a week.

"We can go shopping." Teagan made a face. "I mean, do you own anything besides boring pantsuits and sensible pumps?"

"I have several dresses—"

"In a color other than black, gray or navy?"

Sienna opened her mouth to protest Teagan's criticism and recognized the futility. "Besides, did it ever occur to you that I have clients that I'm supposed to be working for?"

"You can't seriously expect me to believe that their lives will crash down around them if you don't find something boring and old for them to spend their money on."

It was a familiar argument and one that never failed to rub Sienna wrong. "I know you find what I do boring, but just like you have a passion for all things beautiful and trendy, I happen to love finding the perfect pieces of art to add to my clients' collections."

"It's not that I find it boring," Teagan said, "it's just that ever since you went out on your own, you don't make time for me anymore."

Sienna almost laughed out loud at her sister's ridiculous claim. Teagan was the busy one with a rich and active social life, centered in New York City, filled with hangers-on and acquaintances, while Sienna traveled all over the world pursuing artworks. When she went out, she preferred quiet dinners with a few close friends.

"Oh please," Sienna said. "You have plenty of people to hang out with."

"People," Teagan corrected. "Not family."

"Well, that's all about to change." Sienna indicated Dallas Shaw's social media feed. "I guarantee you'll be so happy with your new family that you won't even notice when I leave."

"But what if I don't like them?"

Teagan paused to regard a photo of three generations of Watts family members and Sienna found her gaze drawn to the single anomaly amongst the sea of blond-haired, blue-eyed Southerners. A tall man with tousled mahogany hair stood in the back, his sexy smile hinting at a devil-may-care attitude that kindled her imagination. Something compelling and a little frightening swept across her nerve endings at the strength of her interest.

She shook herself free of his spell. "Then you go back to New York and live your life."

"There's something I haven't told you." Teagan resumed scrolling.

"Like what?"

"I'm not sure I'm returning to New York."

"What?" The anxiety that had been building ever since Teagan announced she'd found her birth family exploded in her chest. "Why not?"

"I've decided I'm going to be the next CEO of Watts Shipping."

Sienna sat in stunned silence while her sister's words played through her mind. The Watts family business was a multimillion-dollar corporation with a fleet of fifty transportation vessels that moved goods all around the world. Founded in the 1920s, they were in the state's top one hundred corporations with nearly fifteen hundred employees worldwide.

While there was no question that Teagan had the Harvard education and the ambition to helm the family company, what she lacked was any knowledge of shipping and the experience needed to run a corporation with annual sales in the hundreds of millions.

"I thought your uncle was the current CEO," Sienna said, "and that one of his sons will be taking over shortly." She pictured the handsome, dark-haired charmer in the family photo, wondering how he'd feel about the competition from the newly arrived outsider.

"Ethan." Teagan scrolled back to the family photo that she'd been looking at earlier. "The thing is, he is adopted and…"

Recognizing where her sister's mind had gone, Sienna controlled a wince. Despite being their father's darling girl and the sole beneficiary of their mother's boundless attention and energy, Teagan defined herself as the adopted child. As if this somehow meant she was less of a Burns than Sienna or their brother, Aiden. The irony of this often led to Sienna wanting to rage at her sister.

As the middle sibling and biological child, Sienna was the one mostly likely to be ignored or excluded. Her brother was expected to take over the family business. Teagan had been the one their mother had adopted because Sienna hadn't been beautiful enough to dress up and show off to Anna's friends. Neither a boy nor a beauty, Sienna had slipped through the cracks of her parents' awareness.

"You think it's your birthright to run the family business," Sienna guessed, thinking how disappointed Teagan had been when despite her superior business skills and suitability to take over the Burns real estate empire, she'd been passed over in favor of Samuel and Anna's biological son, Aiden. "I'm sure you have a shot at it, but is that fair to Ethan?"

"I don't want them to give me the position," Teagan said, but her green eyes took on a frosty glint of remembered disappointment. "I fully intend to earn it. But I want the shot. And I'm going to take it."

"Sure. I guess that's…fair," Sienna said, sympathizing with Ethan now that her sister was poised to claim a position he'd grown up believing was his. "None of this explains why you need me to stay in Charleston beyond a few days. It seems like you're going to have your hands full with getting to know your family as well as Watts Shipping." She said this last with a wry smile that she hoped took the censure out of the words.

"I thought maybe we could work together."

A discordant buzzing filled Sienna's ears. Sometimes the way Teagan's mind worked terrified her. Her sister had embraced their mother's ruthless streak and honed her skills ever since her days of being Queen Bee of their Upper East Side prep school.

"Work together how?"

"You always have such good insights into people. I thought maybe you could help me get to know everyone and figure out my best way in."

"I have clients—" Sienna said, fearful of becoming embroiled in whatever scheme her sister was cooking up.

"Stop using them as an excuse," Teagan snapped, before turning the full power of her pleading expression on Sienna. "I'm sorry. I didn't mean to be such a bitch. I don't want to be all alone down here. You know I need you. Please stay and help me. I'm terrified that I won't fit in and this is when I really need my sister."

"Okay." It was easier to give in than keep resisting. "I don't have anything particularly pressing at the moment."

"Wonderful." Teagan's entire demeanor brightened as it did every time she got her way. "And you never know, you might find some new clients here. Plus, there's tons of museums and you love those."

"I do."

Yet as she gave in, what had promised to be a relaxing interlude amongst Charleston's historic charms vanished like morning mist.

Ethan Watts sat in the living room of his grandfather's elegant estate on the west end of Montague Street a few blocks from the Ashley River. On his phone screen was the email he'd received the night before. Brief and to the point, mysterious and inflammatory, the message had arrived from an anonymous source. Initially he'd dismissed the warning. The sender intended to stir up trouble and Ethan had little patience for the person's shadowy agenda. But he hadn't deleted the email. It described a threat he'd be foolish to ignore.

Teagan Burns intends to become the next CEO of Watts Shipping. She is ruthless and will use every trick in the book to get her way. Watch your back.—A friend

Even as he reread the email for the umpteenth time, Ethan wasn't sure what to make of it. He didn't believe for one second that the anonymous sender was any sort of friend. The sender obviously had an agenda and Ethan refused to trust that he and the person were on the same side.

"I think she's here." For the last twenty minutes his aunt had been watching from the living room windows, anticipating the moment that her long-lost niece would arrive from New York City.

Ethan Watts reached Lenora Shaw's side just as the uniformed driver of the luxury town car got out and circled the vehicle to open the door for his passengers. His aunt vibrated with tension as she awaited her first glimpse of Ava Watts's missing daughter.

Three decades earlier, the headstrong, spoiled youngest daughter of Grady and Delilah Watts had run off to New York against her father's wishes at eighteen. After five years of no contact, Grady had sent an investigator to see what had become of his daughter. Too late, they learned that Ava had died several years before and her infant daughter had been adopted. For twenty-five years the family had been searching for her without success. That hunt ended several months ago when both sides had connected through a genetic testing service database.

Lenora's fingers bit down on Ethan's arm as a petite brunette exited the car. "That can't be her."

"I believe that's Sienna." Based on the research his older brother, Paul, had done on Teagan Burns, Ethan knew this wasn't the missing Watts heiress. "Teagan's older sister."

The woman in question was dressed for business in a simple black pantsuit and white blouse that downplayed her hourglass figure. Neither her long, straight hair, a flat espresso brown, nor the barest of makeup she'd applied to her delicate features and soft lips commanded attention. Unlike her sister, she had a nearly nonexistent social media presence and based on what he noted of her body language and appearance, Sienna Burns obviously preferred to maintain a low profile.

"Oh," Lenora murmured, "there she is."

Ethan tore his gaze away from Sienna in time to witness a pair of long, shapely legs, clad in white high-heel boots, emerging from the town car. Moments later the highly recognizable New York City socialite appeared. A chic blonde "it" girl, who regularly appeared on Page Six and social media, she looked every inch a Manhattan fashionista in a short white romper with navy pinstripes, her gold-blond hair hanging in a silky curtain to her waist.

"She looks exactly like Ava," Lenora said, her tone tight with concern. "Let's hope she doesn't behave like her."

It was no secret that Lenora hadn't gotten along with her willful younger sibling, but Ethan was surprised that Teagan's marked resemblance to her mother had set Lenora off. The entire family had been avidly anticipating this meeting for years. He never imagined a scenario where she wouldn't be fully embraced, but something about his aunt's frown sent a trickle of uneasiness down his spine.

"Why don't we go greet her," Ethan prompted, when his aunt didn't show any signs of moving toward the front door.

Lenora shook off her somber mood and applied a social smile to her lips. "Of course."

The Shaw's housekeeper, Jillian Post, had been standing by and now opened the door to admit the new arrival. Ethan and Lenora reached the broad arch into the wide entry hall just as Teagan crossed the threshold alone. The housekeeper glanced out the door and murmured a question.

"She had something to take care of first," Teagan answered, sounding the tiniest bit peevish.

As the carved front door closed behind her, blocking the June sunshine, the socialite pulled off her enormous sunglasses and gave her surroundings a quick once over before focusing on the pair who'd stepped forward to greet her.

"Hello."

"Welcome to Charleston," Lenora said, taking the lead before things grew awkward. "I'm Lenora Shaw, your aunt, and this is your cousin Ethan."

"It's wonderful to be here." Teagan's lips curved in a picture-perfect smile, but the cool assessment in her eyes as her gaze slid over Ethan sent his thoughts back to that anonymous email. "You were so kind to invite me."

"It's your home," Ethan declared, summoning a beguiling tone to make up for Lenora's less-than-effusive welcome. "We're delighted to have you here."

"Yes, delighted," Lenora echoed while she took in her niece's sophisticated appearance. "Please, come in. Your grandfather will be down shortly."

"Grady's eager to see you," Ethan added. "He's been searching for you for a long time."

"I'm excited to meet him, as well," Teagan said as they all moved into the elegant living room.

Teagan Burns intends to become the next CEO of Watts Shipping.

Ethan scanned Teagan's expression for the duplicity the email warned him about and glimpsed happiness mixed with apprehension. Neither emotion struck him as unusual. The entire family had been buzzing with excitement and nervous energy since they'd learned about Teagan. The meeting was momentous and fraught with tension for all involved. What if they didn't like Ava's daughter or vice versa? What if they all made an immediate connection but Teagan then decided to return to New York City and her busy life there? What if she was a horror and decided to stay in Charleston? How would the family dynamic change?

"Have you been to Charleston before?" Lenora asked, gesturing toward the pale blue damask sofa Ethan had occupied moments before.

"I don't leave New York often," Teagan admitted, as she looked over the space. Was she cataloging the valuables? Trying to decide what she stood to inherit once Grady Watts died? "And when I do, I generally travel to LA or the Caribbean."

"Where's your sister?" Ethan asked, thinking about the woman who'd gotten out of the car first.

Teagan's green eyes snapped to him. "On a business call. She'll join us when she's done."

With conspiracies circling his mind like a pack of

coyotes, Ethan was seized by a sharp need to clear his head. "Why don't I go check on her."

Leaving the two women to get acquainted, Ethan headed outside to see what had become of Sienna Burns. He found her sitting near the bottom of the front steps, her back to the house, an open laptop balanced on her thighs. As he descended toward her, Ethan glanced to where the driver of the town car was unloading a sizable collection of matching cream-colored luggage with champagne leather accents.

"Hello," he said as he drew within earshot of Teagan's sister.

The brunette had been so absorbed in her task that she hadn't noticed his approach. Now, she jerked in surprise, clutching the laptop as it teetered precariously. She turned to stare up at him, but bright afternoon sun splashed across her face, forcing her to squint.

"Oh, hello." She shut her computer as he passed her and slid it into the tote bag near her feet.

When he reached the driveway, he turned to face her. Ethan found his senses tingling with pleasure as he breathed in the sun-warmed scent of vanilla wafting from her. Up close he noted the pale freckles peeking through her foundation and the fact that she'd chewed off her lipstick. But what arrested him was the sharp intelligence in her blue-gray eyes.

"I'm Ethan Watts." To his chagrin, he caught himself smiling in genuine welcome instead of bombarding her with practiced charm. "Teagan's cousin."

"Sienna Burns. Teagan's…sister."

He noted the slight hesitation as she identified her

connection and wondered at it. "Nice to meet you, Sienna Burns."

He held out his hand for her to shake, shocked how eager he was to touch her. Nor was he disappointed when she placed her palm against his, sending an electric charge of awareness zipping through him. From the telltale widening of her eyes and the rising color in her cheeks, he guessed she'd experienced something, as well.

"Nice to meet you," she echoed, making no attempt to take her hand back. In fact, she tilted her torso toward him while her gaze toured his face. Her lips slanted into a grin of feminine appreciation as if she liked what she saw.

This demonstration of mutual attraction set his hormones on fire. Ethan offered her a slow, wolfish smile. He wasn't a stranger to sexual chemistry and enjoyed both a stimulating chase and an easy conquest, but despite the bold appreciation in Sienna's gaze, he suspected that she wasn't going to tumble for his Southern charisma. A challenge then. He was up for that. But then the warning about Teagan popped back into his head.

She...will use every trick in the book to get her way.
Including her sister? The question stopped him cold.

"We've been looking forward to meeting you both," he said, all too aware that he should end the handshake. Instead, he was fighting the desire to slide his thumb over her knuckles. Remembering his manners, he set her free. His skin continued to tingle where it had been in contact with hers.

Sienna absorbed his words with a surprised expression. "Both of us? But I'm not anyone…"

Ethan was struck by her words. Was it false modesty or a bid for sympathy that compelled others to reassure her? "Obviously, you're someone."

"Well, of course." Sienna gave a breathy laugh. "I just mean that Teagan is the star here. I'm just along for the ride."

The way she dismissed her importance left him wondering how often she was compared to her beautiful, stylish sister and found lacking. Ethan understood sibling rivalry. Not that he'd ever gone out of his way to compete against Paul. Likewise, his brother lived in his own world and rarely engaged in such trivial pursuits, but being the second son and an adopted one as well, Ethan had always questioned his place in the family.

Sienna's case was a bit different though. She was the older daughter. The one who'd been born into the Burns family. If anyone would feel as if she belonged, it would be Sienna and not Teagan. Yet Teagan was the one who'd capitalized on the family's social status and wealth while Sienna faded into the background.

At the same time, Sienna was the more approachable of the two. The one he could let his guard down around. She seemed to lack any ulterior motives. The anonymous message had warned him to be wary. Ethan sighed in exasperation. He didn't want to ponder hidden agendas or imagine these women were scheming against him.

"Still, it's good of you to support her," Ethan said.

"I'm sure it wasn't easy to take the time away from your business to accompany her on this visit."

"This is a pretty big deal for her." Sienna slid a lock of hair behind her ear, drawing Ethan's attention to her short, unpainted nails. "For your family as well, I'm sure. Teagan has been looking forward to meeting you all." Mischief flashed in her eyes. "Or should I say all y'all?"

"You speak Southern." He ramped up his drawl, relishing the flirtation.

She looked pleased by his approval. "Just a little. I have a client in New Orleans." She pronounced it New OR-lins like a local. "He's fond of inundating me with Southern colloquialisms whenever we talk."

"Such as?"

"Some of his least colorful are… Kiss my go-to-hell. If that boy had an idea, it would die of loneliness. That dog won't hunt."

"And his more colorful?" Ethan prompted, utterly captivated by the impish glint in her eyes.

"Don't piss on my leg and tell me it's raining." Her cheeks blazed with color that hadn't been there a second earlier. For all her big-city upbringing, she had a trace of shyness that enchanted him.

Could she really be in on Teagan's supposed plans for taking over Watts Shipping? Almost as soon as this notion popped into his head, he pushed it away. And then just as swiftly, he circled back. Dismissing Sienna as a nonparticipant in whatever her sister was cooking up might be the blunder that caused him to lose everything.

Watch your back.

The warning failed to dim his interest in Sienna. Worse, the potential danger in his growing fascination actually enhanced his desire. He was already plotting how to corner her in an isolated place so he could sample her soft lips and seduce her properly. If he thought he'd overcome the reckless streak that had dominated his teens and early twenties, he'd been mistaken. It hadn't been tamed, only sedated.

"Here comes Cory," Ethan said, relieved that his grandfather's caretaker was approaching. "He will take charge of all the luggage." As Sienna got to her feet, Ethan made the introductions. "Cory Post, this is Sienna Burns. She will be staying in the rose guest room. Which of these are yours?"

"That one."

Not surprisingly, she pointed to the single black bag sitting like a crow amongst doves. The hard-sided piece had seen a lot of use.

"You travel light." He shot Sienna a quick glance to confirm. "And quite a bit from the looks of your bag."

"Business trips mostly."

"What sort of business?" he asked, even though thanks to Paul's research, Ethan already knew.

"I'm an independent art consultant."

"That sounds quite interesting. I'll look forward to hearing all about it."

Her long lashes flickered. "It's really quite mundane. A lot of time spent in airplanes and dusty old houses."

"Oh, I'm sure it's not as dull as you make it sound." He leaned toward her with a smile meant to encourage her to give up all her secrets. "I'll bet you've seen some very interesting things. What's your favorite?"

She nibbled her lower lip for a second before answering. "Two years ago, a couple in Toulouse discovered an old painting in their attic after their roof leaked. One of my art world contacts gave me a heads-up so I flew to France to evaluate the painting and it turned out it was the work of the Italian artist Caravaggio."

As she spoke of her discovery, her eyes glowed with enthusiasm, turning what had been a pretty face into something quite breathtaking.

"Fascinating," he murmured, transfixed by the dimples produced by her effervescent smile.

Noting the way his heartbeat stuttered and then started to race, Ethan silently cursed. If that anonymous warning was the real deal, he needed to stay vigilant.

She...will use every trick...

Ethan gave himself a shake. He shouldn't let a stranger get into his head. For all he knew, Teagan had sent the message herself to distract him into chasing shadows. Still, whether Sienna was part of a plot or not, there was much to discover about Teagan's sister and Ethan was looking forward to finding out all about her. Until he did, the challenge would be to keep his attraction hidden from everyone, but especially Teagan. Letting her capitalize on his fascination with Sienna was a risk he couldn't afford.

Two

As Ethan escorted Sienna up the right side of the elegant stone double staircase that curved from the driveway to the front door, she couldn't help but think Teagan wouldn't find him a pushover.

"My family is probably wondering what became of us," he murmured as they slipped through the front door and entered the air-conditioned coolness of the mansion.

"Teagan is quite distracting," Sienna said. "I doubt they've noticed."

The change in temperature and drop in humidity made her conscious of her wrinkled pants and the perspiration coating her skin. In contrast, Ethan seemed impervious to the heat. She inhaled the clean scent of soap that clung to his skin and caught herself smiling. Everything about the man appealed to her.

No doubt a man as handsome and charismatic as Ethan was quite a player. To Sienna's surprise she didn't care. She wasn't planning on tossing her heart into the ring. If she was going to take some time off, she might as well have a little fun of the casual, sensual variety. Ethan might be perfect fling material.

She was floating on a cloud as Ethan guided her into the living room and introduced her to his family. Sienna thanked Teagan's grandfather Grady Watts for his invitation to stay at the house, and then settled back to survey the interaction between Teagan and her biological relatives. Despite the striking family resemblance, there were marked differences in manner.

Teagan and Sienna had been raised by a polished Manhattan socialite and her reserved husband. As approachable as Teagan appeared on social media, in person she could come off as cool or dispassionate. She rarely exhibited the strong feelings that simmered in her. To show such emotion would mar the image of effortless perfection she worked so hard to maintain.

By contrast, Poppy, Lenora and even Grady wore broad smiles and spoke animatedly about Charleston, the rest of the family and all the things they were looking forward to doing with her. Sienna noticed herself getting swept up in their enthusiasm and cheerfulness and was wondering how Teagan was fairing when her sister pulled out her smartphone and began posing with Poppy.

This seemed like a perfect opportunity for Sienna

to slip out. She tugged on Ethan's sleeve and captured his attention.

"Would there be someone who could show me where I'll be staying?" A yawn snuck up on her and she covered the gaff with an embarrassed chuckle. "Sorry. I was hoping to catch a nap on the flight down from New York, but Teagan was too keyed up." Seeing the curiosity in Ethan's gaze, she elaborated. "I flew in from London this morning and didn't get any sleep on the overseas flight."

"I can take you up."

"Thank you."

They made their excuses and headed into a broad hallway that split the house down the middle. Across from the living room was a large formal dining room. While Ethan angled toward the stairs at the far end of the hallway, Sienna poked her head into the room.

"The whole family will be here for dinner tonight," Ethan explained, coming to stand beside her. "They're really excited to meet Teagan."

"How many are coming?"

"My parents, my brother, Paul, and his fiancée, Lia. Aunt Lenora and Uncle Wiley. The twins. You, me and Grady."

"Are you sure I should be there?" Sienna asked, worried that they'd view her as an interloper.

"Of course." Ethan looked surprised that she'd even ask. "You're family, too."

His response warmed her. "The house is really beautiful," Sienna said, retreating into polite chitchat as her emotional reaction caught her off guard.

"Want a quick tour?"

What she wanted was more in time his company. "That'd be great."

He led her into the kitchen and introduced her to Jillian Post, Grady's housekeeper, before showing her the library.

"The house was built in 1804 by Jacob Birch," Ethan said, as they ascended the stairs to the second floor. "Theodore Watts purchased the property in 1898 which is why it's now known as the Birch-Watts Estate. The main house's ninety-four hundred square feet have been remodeled several times, but always with an eye toward preserving and enhancing its Federal style."

"A style that dominated American architecture from 1790 to 1840," she said, aware she was showing off. "The layout is symmetrical with unadorned exteriors." She gestured toward the window where the intricate wrought iron railings that edged the upper terraces could be seen peeping above the windowsill. "Except for the porches and entries. Inside is different with elaborate molded plaster flourishes on the ceilings and borders."

"You know a lot about our architecture," he said, making no effort to cover his surprise.

The approval in Ethan's sexy brown eyes as he shot her a sideways glance sent a shiver of awareness racing over her skin. The photos of him posted on his cousins' social media had sparked her interest. Candid shots of him on a boat, buff and tanned with rippling abs and muscles galore, his hair blowing in the wind, an irrepressible grin on his sculpted lips.

In person, the man possessed the sort of easy, confident charm that women fell for in a hurry. No doubt the guy got a lot of action with the belles of Charleston. And his solicitous behavior since they met gave Sienna the impression that he'd satisfy a woman even as he took care of his own needs. Was it any wonder she was fighting a compelling urge to lick her lips and utter the first naughty double entendre that popped into her mind?

"I make a habit before I travel of reading up on the local history, the art scene, including museums and architecture, and of course the best cuisine." She smiled her thanks as he ushered her into the house. "It gives me a deeper appreciation of the places I visit."

"Do you travel a lot?"

"Generally, I'm on the road three weeks out of four." A choice that kept her from dwelling on a growing dissatisfaction with her lack of a personal life.

"Sounds lonely."

Her lips twisted into a wry grimace. "I work so much that I really don't notice."

"So there's no special someone waiting to welcome you home?"

Sienna couldn't meet Ethan's candid gaze. "Um, no one at all, actually."

She hadn't been kidding about how much she worked. Dating was both time-consuming and an energy drain. When she did venture out, she'd yet to meet a man whose companionship she craved, and if she was in the mood for sex, she had a straightforward way of scratching that itch. Unfortunately, this left her woefully ill-equipped when it came to the nuances of flirting and seduction.

On the second floor he indicated his grandfather's room and the one where Teagan would be staying.

"It was her mother's room," he added as they peeked into the sunny yellow room with green-and-white-floral draperies and comforter. "Looks like Cory delivered her luggage. Yours should be in your room, as well."

Side by side they ascended to the third floor. These stairs were narrower than the lower levels and forced Sienna into closer proximity with the Charleston charmer. She stumbled and Ethan caught her elbow to steady her. She smiled to thank him, shocked by how her heart pounded at his touch.

"This is your room." He indicated a sunny space, tucked beneath the eves with slanting walls painted an inviting rose.

The room had been furnished with a four-poster bed and a cozy love seat placed under a window with a view of rooftops and a steeple of one of Charleston's many churches.

"This is lovely." Sienna set her laptop case down and barely restrained the urge to throw herself on the bed and groan in pleasure. "Thank you."

"I hope you'll let me show you around Charleston while you're here," Ethan said, his alluring smile awakening an irresistible urge to grin back. "Our city has a lot to offer."

His deep voice resonated through her like a summer thunderstorm, leaving Sienna caught up in the midst of a wild and turbulent squall.

"That would be lovely," she murmured, catching herself staring at his lips and wondering if his kisses would be slow and sweet or hot and feverish.

His even white teeth flashed in a satisfied smile that was just shy of smug as he pulled out his phone. "Let me give you my number so you can call me when you get a free moment."

Sienna keyed his number into her contacts, and then at his urging she called him so he had her number, as well. The moment had come for them to part, but Sienna couldn't bring herself to make the first move.

"I'll leave you to unpack." He gave her a bone-melting smile. "And nap. We meet for cocktails before dinner. See you at seven."

"See you."

Left by herself, Sienna collapsed onto the comfortable bed and blew the air from her lungs. She glanced down at the phone in her hand, shivering as she regarded Ethan's contact information. Seconds later, she cued up her favorites list and dialed a familiar number.

"We made it to Charleston," she declared when her best friend, Gia Milani, answered. Both art history majors, the women had met as college freshmen and were often mistaken as sisters because of their similar coloring and strong bond.

"How's the family?" Gia asked.

"I've only met a few of them, but they seem nice."

Ethan's broad shoulders and mesmerizing gaze popped into her mind. What sort of hell was her ambitious sister going to put him through as Teagan made her bid to take over the running of the family's international shipping business? She sighed.

Gia must've picked up on her angst because she asked, "What's wrong?"

"I think Teagan is planning on staying in Charleston."

"For how long?"

"Maybe for good." For the first time since her sister dropped the bombshell, Sienna gave her reaction a chance to breathe. The anxiety was stronger than she would've predicted. These days she barely saw her sister. What did it matter if Teagan was here or in New York City? "She has this crazy idea that she deserves to be the next CEO of the family's shipping business."

"Is this because your dad picked Aiden over her to run Burns Properties?"

"It has a lot to do with it, but I don't think that's her only reason." Sienna thought about the comment Teagan had made about Ethan being adopted. "Long before Dad passed her over, she was hung up on this whole issue of not being a Burns by blood. And now that she's found her blood relatives, I think she believes it will all be different."

"You've met them. What do you think?"

"She might be right. I mean the family resemblance is striking. And they're thrilled that she's here."

Gia paused for a beat as she absorbed Sienna's response. "How are you feeling?"

"Me?" Sienna let loose a shaky laugh. "I'm great. Teagan asked me to stick around for longer than I'd planned so I'm going to be staying in Charleston for a week or so."

"You're finally taking time off and plan to spend it with Teagan?" Her friend sounded all kinds of surprised and disappointed.

Sienna didn't blame her. Gia hadn't understood why Sienna had agreed to go with Teagan to meet her Charleston family in the first place. Although Gia was a wonderful sounding board for most of Sienna's problems, when it came to her relationship with Teagan, Gia had very strong opinions.

"It's a vacation. From what I've seen of it, Charleston is nice. And I could use a break."

"Okay." But Gia didn't make it sound like she was on board with Sienna's decision.

"What's wrong?"

"I just don't get why Teagan wanted you there in the first place."

Irritation flared even as Sienna recognized that she'd wondered the same thing. When Teagan had initially extended the invitation, Sienna had been too thrilled to be asked and hadn't considered her sister's motivation.

"Moral support," Sienna offered, wanting this to be true.

"I hope you're right," Gia said. "I'd hate to think she was involving you in some scheme."

"The only thing she has on her mind at the moment is making a good impression on her family."

"And taking over as CEO of Watts Shipping."

"Well, sure, but there's no way I can be of help there."

Gia hummed thoughtfully. "Maybe not. Just do me a favor and watch your back, okay?"

Ethan made sure to sit beside Sienna at dinner. He intended to get to know her a lot better and hopefully figure out her sister's plans in the process. Tonight, while Teagan wore a sequined, thigh-baring frock, with sheer sleeves, that could've graced any red-carpet event, Sienna paired black, wide-legged trousers with a modest white lace blouse. While her sister had chosen to pair chandelier earrings with her wild golden mane that framed her beautiful face, Sienna had opted for a severe, sleek look by pulling her long hair into a low ponytail and fastening small diamond studs to her earlobes.

Various family members peppered Teagan with questions about her life in New York, including her successful jewelry line and makeup concierge businesses as well as the various celebrities she'd been photographed with. Ethan noticed Sienna made no attempt to join the conversation.

"Were you able to sleep?" he asked, the images of her stretched out on the bed in the upstairs guest room sending a series of steamy pictures drifting through his mind.

"Can you still see the waffle pattern from the blanket?" She touched her cheek in a charmingly unselfconscious gesture. "I swear I was only going to close my eyes for a second and the next thing I knew two hours went by."

"Are you feeling more rested?"

"Yes, thank you." Her lips curved in a secret smile. "I think the reality of being on vacation is starting to take hold. If I'm not careful, my clients will think I've abandoned them."

Could she possibly be as uncomplicated as she appeared? Was she simply a hardworking art curator who parlayed her Upper East Side connections into a lucrative career? The dossier Paul had prepared on Teagan touched only briefly on her other family members' financial situations and public personas. In Sienna's case, the information was limited to her professional website and several references in art-related articles.

After meeting both Burns sisters, he'd understood the warning delivered by the anonymous emailer where Teagan was concerned. But did Sienna's fleeting smiles and quiet reserve hide a truly devious mind? It was hard to believe, yet didn't that make her all the more dangerous?

"I guess while you're visiting us, I'm gonna have to make sure you rest and play." Ethan bumped his shoulder against hers in a friendly gesture.

"That's kind of you, but I can't take you away from business." Was she playing hard to get to lure him in? If so, it was working. "And what I have planned would probably bore you to tears."

Given the strength of his interest, he doubted that. "You might be surprised."

"I'm going to visit every museum in Charleston and acquaint myself with all the Southern artists represented there."

"I have to confess something." Lowering his voice, he leaned her way in a conspiratorial manner and was rewarded by the rosy flush that stained her cheeks. "I've never been in half the museums in this town. That's a shame, wouldn't you say?"

Her blue-gray eyes lost a little of their sparkle as she surveyed his face as if to gauge his motives for flirting with her. Why would she do that? Couldn't she feel the electricity between them? Without breaking eye contact, he took inventory of the women seated around the table. Sienna Burns was not the most beautiful or stylish of them, but beneath her calm exterior he sensed she sizzled with passion and determination. He just had to figure out the best way to focus that fervor on him, and the key to figuring out her sister's plans would be in his grasp.

"I wouldn't want to monopolize all your time," Sienna demurred, her elusiveness a lure he couldn't resist.

"I wasn't just being polite earlier when I offered to show you around," he said. "I wouldn't want you to leave Charleston with less than the best impression of our fair city."

"Well then, I accept."

Satisfied that he'd successfully initiated step one of his divide-and-conquer plan, Ethan glanced toward Teagan and found her watching his interaction with Sienna. He thought he noted the tiniest trace of speculation in her green gaze. Catching her eye, he smiled and inclined his head to acknowledge her interest. The

corner of her mouth twitched before she turned away
to respond to a question his cousin Dallas had asked.

After dinner, when the family settled into the cozy
library with its red walls and comfortable seating,
Ethan offered to take Sienna for a walk around the
grounds. Her gaze flicked to where the twins flanked
Teagan on the blue velvet sofa, the blonde trio so similar in appearance that they looked more like sisters
than cousins. Sienna's expression grew pensive, and
a familiar stab of angst pierced his chest. As the only
dark-haired member of a family of blonds, he knew
what it felt like to be an outsider.

Ethan doubted anyone noticed their departure as he
guided her out the French doors that led to the side terrace, down a circular, wrought iron staircase and onto
the brick walkway that ran the length of the house.
They had a choice of several paths that led off through
the gardens, toward the pool or the dwellings at the
back of the property.

"The estate occupies a little over an acre," he nar-
rated as they ambled past formal beds filled with
boxwood and flowers. "And includes the main house,
carriage and caretaker houses. The twins occupy the
latter if you're ever looking for them."

"An acre is a lot of land for downtown Charleston,
isn't it?"

"Over the years Grady was able to purchase some
of the surrounding buildings that were original to the
property and redesign the grounds."

The deep gold of fading sunshine filtered through
the lush plantings as Ethan kept pace with Sienna's

slow amble along the gravel path. She murmured in delight at the mix of formal and free-style design that took a landscape team several hours to maintain each week. Since his knowledge was limited to a few well-known flowering plants, he spent his time pondering the best way to approach her.

Maybe at first Ethan had expected to engage her in a rousing duel of clever questions designed to trick her into revealing her sister's plans. But watching the way her fingertips skimmed over shiny leaves and delicate flower petals, he revised his strategy. Throwing her off-balance by exploiting her latent sensuality would be way more entertaining.

He'd never had fantasies about a sexy librarian before and although he'd heard that the brain was an important sexual organ, he was usually more interested in a woman's body from the neck down. Now, however, as he drank in the soft floral scent of Sienna's perfume and noticed the way she nibbled her lip when deep in thought, he suspected he'd been missing out. Ethan was abruptly besieged by images of her in a fitted pencil skirt, her full breasts straining the buttons of a snug white blouse. The fantasy look was completed by sexy, sky-high heels and ugly black glasses that she could whip off as her long, dark hair came tumbling out of a tidy topknot.

Holy...wow!

"Did you bring a swimsuit?" he asked as they reached the open space where the pool glowed like a turquoise jewel. "Dallas and Poppy do paddleboard yoga in the mornings. Lia got them started when she first came here to help my grandfather recover from his stroke. I'm sure they'd be thrilled if you and Teagan joined them."

"I'll mention it to her." Sienna hesitated before adding, "Regarding Lia… I have a question."

Tension gripped him at her curiosity. Their easy interaction had made him relax his vigilance.

"Fire away."

"I don't want to overstep your family's warm welcome, but I have to ask…" Sienna's gaze was fixed on the open-air pool house; she seemed to be gathering her thoughts. "Before dinner when I asked Lia how she and Paul met, she told me a rather startling story."

Here was evidence of the two-pronged Burns sisters attack. Sienna dug up the dirt and passed it to Teagan to exploit. Still, it wasn't as if he was the only person with knowledge of how Lia had come to be involved with his family.

"Grady was going downhill fast after his stroke and his greatest wish was to see his granddaughter before he died. I convinced Lia to pretend to be his long-lost granddaughter, thinking this would make him happy."

Her eyes went round. "So it's true. I'm sorry, but that's an extraordinary thing to do."

"At the time it seemed like a simple plan," he admitted. "One that was supposed to ease an old man's heart." Ethan shook his head as he recalled just how complicated the situation had become. "But Lia is a miracle worker. She spent a few days with my grandfather and he rallied."

"So your brother mentioned." Sienna was eyeing him keenly.

"Paul just about killed me when he came back from a conference and found out what I'd done." Despite the strain the stunt had put on their relationship, Ethan didn't regret the scheme. Because of it, Paul was in love with a wonderful woman and happier than he'd ever been.

"But he had to be delighted at your grandfather's unexpected recovery."

"Of course, and the happy outcome is that he and Lia are getting married."

"Yet it wasn't all that simple at the time."

"I suppose it was a little uncomfortable for Paul to be falling for someone while pretending to be her first cousin."

A little uncomfortable? Ethan knew Paul had gone through hell. He just couldn't bring himself to feel bad about it. Grady was thriving. It had prompted them to try to locate their actual missing relative through a genetic testing service, and once they'd found Teagan, Ethan had decided to take a test of his own to see if his birth family was out there somewhere and looking for him.

"How did everything come out in the open?" Sienna asked, dragging Ethan's thoughts back to the conversation.

"Why are you so curious about the story?"

"I was just wondering what sort of an impact the situation would have on your family accepting Teagan. After all, they fell in love with Lia after thinking she was your cousin. Will they be more cautious when it comes to Teagan?"

It was a valid question. "I don't know. I mean, everyone was delighted to hear that we'd found Ava's real daughter. No one has mentioned any reservations to me. As far as I can tell, they have every intention of fully embracing her. Why do you ask?"

"Teagan doesn't show her emotions very often, but I know she has high hopes for becoming part of this family. I don't want her to be disappointed."

"I think you could see from how dinner went tonight that you don't need to worry about that. Teagan is a Watts through and through."

Sienna looked somewhat mollified. "You've been so kind to show me the grounds, but I should probably be getting back."

"It's been my pleasure," Ethan declared, surprised how reluctant he was to part ways. "And I meant what I said earlier about showing you around Charleston. Let's start by having dinner tomorrow night."

"Okay."

"Wonderful."

Pleasure flared at her quick acceptance. "I'll pick you up at six."

They returned to the house in the fading light. At the bottom of the stairs that spiraled up to the side terrace, he bid her good-night.

"Thank you for making me feel welcome." Her hand rested on his sleeve for too brief a second.

Lightning flashed along his nerve endings at the barely-there contact. "Of course."

"Good night."

Given his body's agitation, Ms. Sienna Burns appeared to have won this round. Teeth grinding, he let his gaze linger on her departing form a heartbeat too long before heading for his car.

Watch your back.

Wise words, but Ethan wasn't sure his back was the part of him in danger.

Three

Sienna was seated with her laptop on the comfy love seat by the window when Teagan entered her room without knocking. She'd been reviewing an art collection that was being auctioned off in Salzburg in two weeks and making a list of the pieces that might interest her clients.

"We need to go shopping," Teagan announced, homing in on Sienna's closet like a fashion-seeking missile. Paying no attention to her sister's objections, Teagan threw open the door, gave the contents a disgusted glance before turning to face Sienna. "Everything that we brought from New York is all wrong."

Knowing it was fruitless to argue, Sienna looked up from her laptop and sighed. "You may have packed the wrong things, but everything I brought is perfectly

fine." Ignoring her sister's disparaging snort, Sienna
continued. "And for that matter, so is everything you
brought. You're just looking for an excuse to go shopping."

Teagan's expression spoke volumes. "I never have to
look for an excuse to buy clothes. And you know I'm
right." Teagan was wearing a loose-fitting white crop
top, floral midi skirt and black-and-white colorblock
pumps. With red lipstick, blond hair sleeked back into
a low ponytail and chunky earrings, she looked ready
to lunch at La Grenouille. "Everything that I brought
looks too New York. I stand out and that's the last thing
I'm trying to do."

"For once," Sienna muttered, too low and too fast
for Teagan to catch.

"I don't want my family to think, there's the girl
from New York City, every time they look at me. I
want to fit in. I want them to think, hey, she belongs
in Charleston."

A brand-new email popped into Sienna's inbox, taking her attention away from her sister. She'd sent several images from the upcoming Salzburg auction to
one of her bigger clients and he'd gotten back to her.

"Could you please stop working for five minutes
and talk to me?" Teagan demanded.

"Is this still about you taking over at Watts Shipping?" Sienna asked, scanning the message before typing a quick reply.

"Of course. How can I convince them to consider
me for the position if I don't look as if I'm planning

on staying in Charleston? I need to look like I'm assimilating."

As uncomfortable as Sienna was with her sister's plan, she couldn't argue with the logic. Appearances counted. A fact that had been thrown in her face starting when she was old enough to dress herself.

First it had been her mother's despair that no matter how much she spent on Sienna's clothes, the high-end designer fashions look frumpy on her. Then came high school where even though they wore uniforms, the truly fashionable stood out. Whether it was a trendy haircut, the way they styled their jewelry or the shoes they wore, something about the influencers set them apart.

Needless to say, Teagan was one of the trendsetters while Sienna, who'd never been confident about her looks, had faded into the background.

"Well, you're right about fitting in," Sienna said. "You'd better go shopping. Have fun."

Expecting that this would send Teagan on her way, Sienna was caught off guard when her sister planted her palm on the cover of the laptop and snapped it shut. Sienna yanked her hands back just in time to avoid a solid rap on her knuckles.

"Hey!" she complained. "What's the big idea?"

"You're coming with us."

"When you say us…?" Sienna asked, reluctantly setting aside her laptop. "Who else is coming?"

"Dallas and Poppy, of course," she said, naming the twins. "And Paul's fiancée, Lia."

Sienna had watched her sister operate before. Every

time she found herself in a new situation, she gathered people to her cause, charming, bribing or blackmailing them into assisting, whichever worked best. In this case, she needed to avoid making enemies, so charm and bribery it was.

"Sounds like you'll have plenty of people offering opinions." And of course, bestowing compliments. "You don't really need me."

"Of course I need you." Teagan reached down and clamped her hand on Sienna's arm, tugging her to her feet. "I know you'll give me your honest opinion."

Sienna snorted. "You want my opinion about fashion?" She crossed her arms and leveled a hard stare at her sister. "What's your real reason for wanting me along?"

"Okay, fine. I knew you wouldn't come if I told you that I want to go shopping to buy you some new clothes. I know what you're gonna say," she rushed on, holding up her hand to forestall Sienna's protests. "But honestly, there's not a flattering outfit in there. You need some clothes that accentuate your curves instead of hiding them, and a whole lot more color."

Sienna glanced down at her serviceable navy pants and white shirt. It wasn't that Sienna didn't care how she looked; it was more that she'd hated being compared to her glamorous, fashion-influencer sister and had stopped trying to keep up with Teagan a long time ago.

"I don't see the point in spending a bunch of money on things I won't wear to work."

Teagan waved her sister's objections away. "It

wouldn't kill you to add some stylish pieces to your work wardrobe." Looping her arm through Sienna's, Teagan snagged her sister's purse and drew her out of the room. "Besides, you need a few things to wear while you're down here. Honestly, no one will give you a second look if you don't make an effort."

"Why do I care if anyone gives me a second look?" Sienna asked.

Yet although it pained her to admit it, Sienna was delighted to be included. In New York, Teagan had a hundred distractions. Between her hectic social life and three flourishing businesses, no one received Teagan's full attention.

"You need it because I saw the way you were looking at Ethan," Teagan said with a sly smile. "You're attracted to him and if you want him to notice you, you need to put on a pretty dress, fix your hair and apply a little makeup."

Sienna's face went hot. "I am not interested in Ethan."

"Oh, don't even," Teagan interrupted with zeal. "You were looking at him like he was a chocolate cake and you wanted to devour every bite."

Remembering his smile, the electric zing of attraction when he'd taken her hand, Sienna opened her mouth to deny it again, but they'd reached the second floor and she was afraid the exchange would be overheard.

"If it motivates you," Teagan said, "I think he's interested in you, too. You'd make a cute couple."

"I don't think I'm his type," Sienna protested, hoping Teagan wouldn't give the matter another thought.

Her sister was so accustomed to being the center of attention that when someone showed an interest in Sienna, Teagan turned on the charm. She didn't do it on purpose, but with her looks and vivacious personality she was the sun that the rest of them revolved around.

"You don't think you're any man's type," her sister countered. "But you and I know that's not true."

In truth, several men had found her attractive. Unfortunately, once they met Teagan, they'd found her far more appealing.

"And I think he's into you, as well," Teagan confided, as they reached the door that led to the back terrace and the stairs to the extensive gardens between the back of the house and the garage.

While they were visiting, Teagan and Sienna had been offered the use of one of several vehicles gathering dust in Grady's garage since his stroke many months ago.

"Where are we headed?" Sienna asked, sliding into the passenger seat. She would've preferred to be the one behind the wheel—Teagan rarely got out of New York City to practice her driving skills—but her sister liked being in control.

"Poppy is working so I thought we'd swing by her salon and pick her up."

Sienna should've realized something was up, but until she was herded into a stylist chair, she hadn't realized the reason they stopped at Poppy's salon was so that she could be bullied into having her hair cut and highlighted. While Teagan and her cousin discussed Sienna as if she was a shabby doll rather than a living, breathing woman, Sienna sipped white wine and surrendered to the transformation. An hour and a half later, she stared at her reflection, marveling at the caramel highlights and wavy layers that added volume and dimension to her hair.

"You have gorgeous hair," Poppy said, obviously pleased with herself. "Your cut just needed to be freshened up a little bit."

A little bit was an understatement. Finishing up her second glass of wine, Sienna stared at her reflection and barely recognized herself. Had she really avoided competing with Teagan to the extent that she'd stopped trying to look her best? Apparently so, because the smiling woman reflected back at her appeared not just beautiful but also happy about it.

Feeling a little off-balance, Sienna got up from the chair and tried to pay Poppy.

The hairdresser laughed and waved her off. "You're family. And family doesn't pay."

Determined to find a way to repay Poppy's kindness, Sienna exited the salon and followed the other women down the street to begin their shopping. What followed was a blur of wine, women and far too much fashion for Sienna to keep it all straight. Not long after she was halfway through her third glass of wine that afternoon, Dallas and Lia showed up to offer their opinions. The quartet kept putting more outfits in the dressing room for Sienna to try on, barely giving her space to notice that she modeled five outfits to one of theirs.

In the end, after repeating the routine in several more stores, she exited the final one having spent more money on clothes in a single afternoon than in the whole of last year. They swung by the car to drop off her purchases and then headed to the twins' favorite watering hole with rooftop seating. Dallas had worked in several award-winning kitchens around Charleston and was well-known in the restaurant scene. When the bartender spied her leading their group in, he sent over a specialty cocktail for them all to try. As Sienna sipped the delicious fruity martini, she surveyed the view and savored being one of Teagan's posse. Of course, she reflected, it wouldn't last. Her sister did nothing out of the goodness of her heart. If she dragged Sienna shopping, there would be a motive behind her actions. It was only a matter of time before the purpose was revealed.

"To Sienna's new look," Teagan began, lifting her glass in a festive gesture. "Here's hoping a certain someone will notice."

While the other three echoed the toast, Teagan locked eyes with Sienna and smirked. Even though she'd been expecting it, Sienna shivered in dread at her sister's Machiavellian manipulation. Obviously, Teagan intended to throw Sienna at Ethan, but to what purpose? Nor could she demand an answer from her sister. Teagan was a slippery eel when it came to admitting she was up to anything. Sienna would just have to keep her eyes open and hope when the ax fell that she saw it coming soon enough to get out of its way.

Ethan bounded up the front steps of his grandfather's home, eager to spend the evening with Sienna Burns, and find out what she knew about her sister's plans. He found her seated at the dining room table, her laptop open, her fingers flying over the keys. His initial thought was that she hadn't been kidding about being a workaholic. His second impression took longer to coalesce. As his gaze skimmed over her, his senses came online, so that his body—not his mind—dominated his reaction to her transformation.

Someone—he guessed his cousin Poppy—had transformed Sienna's long hair to better enhance the creamy perfection of her skin. Gone was the low ponytail of forgettable brown. Instead, wavy strands of rich chocolate, threaded with caramel, framed her oval face and drew attention to her blue-gray eyes and plump lips.

And the changes didn't end there. Her utilitarian uniform of dark pants and white top had been replaced by a floral organza dress in peach-and-coral tones that enhanced her abundant curves. Ruffles fluttered along the V of her neckline, drawing attention to the swell of her breasts and offering eye-popping glimpses of her ample cleavage. She looked feminine, approachable, absurdly kissable. He wanted to wrap his fingers around her small waist and pull her tight against his body. To savor the lavish delights of her pillowy breasts squashed against his chest.

Holy hell! He was getting aroused just looking at her.

Ethan caught hold of himself and wrestled his expression into easy congeniality. It would not serve his plans to scare the girl right off the bat by leering at her like a man who was only after her body. He'd save that for later in the evening.

"Hey," he said, his voice sounding rusty. He swallowed and tried again. "Are you ready to go?"

"Just about," she said without looking up from the laptop screen. "I have a client who wants a piece that's going up for auction in a couple of weeks and I'm trying to gage the level of interest out there so I can give him an idea how much it might go for."

"Take your time," he murmured, content to trail his gaze over her for a few more unguarded minutes. "I like your dress."

"Thank you." She made a face, but whether it was about what she was typing or his compliment, he couldn't tell.

"Is it new?"

"Yes." Her gaze finally slid his direction. "Why do you ask?"

The look in her eyes as she surveyed him in turn was a gut punch he didn't see coming. Appreciation made her lips curve just the tiniest bit. As his heart beat harder, he wasn't sure if he should resist his attraction or channel it into his plot to use seduction to uncover her sister's plans. If not for that damned email, he could see himself having fun with Sienna. Her blend of intel-

ligence and artlessness was a fascinating combination
he was eager to explore.

With Teagan, every facial expression and word she
spoke seemed practiced and prepared. Behind her
beautiful green eyes he'd spied a shrewd brain that
plotted and planned. That was why after meeting her,
he'd had no trouble believing the anonymous emailer's claim that she intended to battle him for control
of Watts Shipping.

Sienna was much harder to figure out. One moment she was blushing at something that had passed
between them. The next she looked like she'd enjoy a
lusty romp in the bedroom. And just when he thought
he'd figured her out, she threw her intelligence at him
and retreated behind a wall of facts and candid observation. Had he ever met a woman this complex? Which
facets represented the real Sienna Burns and how did
he exploit them to his advantage?

"Because," Ethan said, realizing he'd taken too long
to answer, "I can see the price tag."

"Oh." She began a frantic search that was equal
parts comical and charming.

Ethan cursed to himself even as his lips curved into
a grin. If his intention was to seduce her, he should've
slid his fingers up her side to indicate where the tag
was. His touch that close to the swell of her breast
would no doubt have a predictable effect on them both.
Instead, he stayed rooted to the spot and enjoyed the
show as she twisted and turned, offering him an eye-
ful of cleavage that lay previously hidden beneath the
floral ruffles.

There was no way he'd make it through the night without getting his hands on her.

While she retreated to the kitchen to find scissors, he glanced at her open laptop. A quick perusal of her email exposed no damning messages between her and Teagan or anyone else for that matter. Not that he expected there to be. Surely they were clever enough to cover their tracks.

In minutes Sienna returned to the dining room, the hem of her floral dress fluttering about her knees, drawing Ethan's attention to her shapely calves. She was barefoot, having abandoned her coral-colored sandals beneath the table. They were beyond easy reach and she would have to crawl under the table to fetch them.

"Let me get those," he said, dropping to his knee before she could. Snagging the straps, he pulled them out and arranged the shoes before her feet, glancing at her smooth, pale legs as he did so.

"Thanks," she murmured huskily, biting her lip as if unsure what to do about his apparent interest.

"My pleasure." He'd never spoken more truthfully.

As if disconcerted by the fact that he didn't immediately rise, she plopped down on the chair where she'd been sitting before. His current position at her feet was too close to enable her to fasten the straps so they stared at each other for an awkward beat before he stood and stepped back.

Proximity to her made his stomach pitch oddly. The sensation was magnified when she glanced up at him from beneath her lashes. Her expression, an intriguing mixture of curiosity, concern and confusion, rocked him back on his heels. Either this was a big act or she was unlike any woman he'd ever been attracted to.

When it came to sex, he liked his partners experienced and willing. He didn't want to worry about awkwardness or hurt feelings in the aftermath. Usually that wasn't a problem for him. He had a reputation around Charleston for being an impossible catch.

He'd already decided to exert all his charm on Sienna and hope she trusted him enough to relax her guard and talk about her sister's plans. What remained open-ended was how far to take things. Sleeping with her might be the highlight of his busy social schedule, but he wasn't sure he could trust himself to remain indifferent.

"Are you ready to go?" he asked.

"Let me run my laptop back to my room and grab my purse."

While he waited, Ethan pulled out his phone and reflected on the latest message from the anonymous sender.

Sienna is very adept at reading people. Be careful how much you tell her.—A friend

The reason this particular warning bothered him had little to do with the content of the message and more that his anonymous "friend" seemed to have an inside track on Ethan's activities. Who could be behind it? He doubted it was someone close to him. Anyone in his life who had his best interest at heart would know to come to him directly rather than go all clandestine with sinister warnings.

Nor was this particular advice earth-shattering. Ethan rarely trotted out his thoughts and feelings to those he trusted. He wasn't about to give away the store to someone he'd just met.

By the time Sienna returned, Ethan had settled on his strategy. They would head to a romantic restaurant where he would order wine and ply her with delicious seafood and a decadent dessert. Then, with her lulled by great food and scintillating conversation, they would stroll under the moonlight where, with the table no longer a barrier between them, he would offer tantalizing hints of the sexual pleasures that awaited her. All leading to the eventual spilling of her secrets in the sweaty daze of postlovemaking bliss.

Four

They passed through a wrought iron gate and navigated a meandering brick pathway bordered by densely planted landscaping to get to the restaurant Ethan had chosen. To Sienna, it felt like stepping into a hidden garden. Inside, a mix of old and new offered a cozy ambiance. Large contemporary chandeliers warmed the oyster-toned, velvet-lined walls hung with hundred-year-old portraits. The effect was inviting and Sienna couldn't wait to see the menu.

The hostess escorted them to a quiet table for two in the back corner. As Sienna settled onto the banquette seat that ran the length of the restaurant's back wall, she realized that while she had a view of the entire restaurant, Ethan's only scenery was her. This proved im-

mediately disconcerting as he set aside his menu and
brought the full power of his attention to bear.

"Is this place okay?" Ethan was behaving like a perfect gentleman, a swoon-worthy date, bringing her to
a romantic restaurant, checking in to make sure she
was happy.

"It's perfect." *You're perfect.* Too perfect. Yet, she
was hopelessly ignoring the red flag flapping in her
face.

"Wonderful." His alluring smile sent butterflies
whisking over her nerve endings. "I want your first
dinner out to be memorable."

"Oh, I'm sure it will be that," she murmured, mentally removing his linen jacket and slipping the buttons
of his white shirt loose one by one.

Charleston's sultry heat left her craving endless
hours of sweaty, energetic, creative sex with a man
who made her feel like the most beautiful woman on
the planet.

Ethan Watts fit the bill.

"Good." He drawled the word, the vowels lingering
decadently on his lips and tongue.

Sienna sipped water and resisted the urge to fan
herself. She wasn't accustomed to being wooed. Or
maybe it was better to say that she wasn't comfortable
being romanced. The only way she'd found to keep
her heart from being broken was to remain in charge
of whom she dated and when she slept with someone.
For the most part she chose unsophisticated men with
no connections to her career who were wildly romantic. It was hard to take men like that seriously and she

was able to enjoy their bodies without ever engaging her mind or heart.

That's what made Ethan so dangerous.

The last of her restraint was fraying beneath his outrageous flirting and come-hither gazes. Not only was she dying to get her hands on his gorgeous body, but she was also keenly aware of the sharp mind beneath his flagrant charm. Hot and smart was a combination destined to inspire a whole host of needs. And there were so many.

"To the first of many visits you'll make to Charleston," Ethan said, extending his wineglass toward her. Since they'd both decided on the blue crab ravioli, he'd suggested a bottle of Châteauneuf-du-Pape Blanc.

"To firsts." She breathed in the wine's peach and floral scents before taking a sip. Fruity and fresh with notes of honey, the white wine slipped along her tongue, making her smile. "Oh, this is delicious."

"I'm glad you like it." His deep, rich voice had a rumbling sort of purr that wove pictures in her mind of long, slow kisses and his hands skimming over her heated naked flesh. "Would you like to start with the muscles?"

"Um." Sienna blinked. "Sure." Having no idea what she'd just agreed to, she lifted her wineglass again and set it to her lips.

"It's my favorite appetizer on the menu."

Oh. Mussels. Not muscles. Amused and all too aware she was blushing, she shifted uncomfortably in her seat. It didn't help that Ethan watched her with narrowed eyes as if he could read every nuance of her expression.

"Sounds great."

To her relief, the waiter approached and took their dinner orders. This brief respite gave her enough breathing space to regain her composure. After he left, she took control of the conversation.

"What was it like growing up in Charleston?"

"I have to think it was like growing up anywhere." His throwaway answer was telling. He didn't want to talk about himself. "School, friends and family. I think you've already figured out we're a close-knit group."

"I have, and it seems as if you all have embraced Teagan as one of you own." Sienna paused to consider her next words. She didn't want to be disloyal to her sister, but at some point, Teagan's true nature was going to show. "She isn't quite as laid-back as you all are so I hope you're ready for her to bring her New York energy to your Southern city."

"I think she'll be a good influence on my cousins. She's very driven and they could use a little of that."

"Oh she's driven," Sienna said, trying to keep the irony out of her voice. "And so it seems are you and Paul."

"Paul is in a league of his own." The pride in Ethan's voice was at odds with his sardonic smile, suggesting that the brothers had a complicated relationship. "He's always been obsessed with computers and of course no one in our family has any idea what it is that he does, except that he does it very well."

"The two of you are the only ones who live outside

downtown Charleston, right?" Sienna found it interesting that the siblings had chosen to distance themselves from the rest of the family. "And both of you are on the water."

"Paul's Isle of Palms house is on the beach, but I like to spend as much time on the water as I can drinking beer and fishing with my buddies. My house has access to the river where I step out my back door and onto my boat."

Her phone buzzed in her purse and she made an involuntary move to pull it out before remembering that she deserved this night off.

"I guess that enjoying boating makes sense for a man whose family runs an international shipping company," she said, determined to keep her attention focused on Ethan.

"I got my love of the water from Grady. He keeps a cruiser at the yacht club. Anyone in the family can use it, but I'm the only one who does."

When her phone sounded again, Sienna ground her teeth and wished she'd turned the damned thing off before leaving for the restaurant.

"Do you need to get that?" Ethan asked, showing no annoyance at the interruption.

"I really don't."

"But you want to?"

Sienna shook her head. "It's more that I suffer from a Pavlovian reaction to any noise my phone makes. Since I deal with clients and art dealers both here and abroad, it isn't unusual for them to reach out to me at all times of the day and night. Usually, I jump on every communication. But tonight, I'm totally focused on you."

His delighted grin let her know she'd said the perfect thing. Sienna found herself wishing she was seated on his lap, running her fingers through his thick, dark hair.

"You are really dedicated to what you do." He cocked his head. "Do you love it that much?"

"I love the treasure-hunting aspect of it. Seeing the thrill on my client's face when I secure something beautiful for them makes the long hours worthwhile."

"You're lucky to do something that makes you happy."

"I am, although sometimes I dread the idea of getting on another airplane."

"Have you considered staying in one place and curating for a museum?"

"Sometimes. Or I think about finishing my art history PhD and teaching somewhere."

"What's stopping you?"

Sienna grimaced. "The idea of standing up in front of a room full of college students and watching their eyes glaze over as I lecture."

"I can see where that might not be ideal, but surely you could use your credentials in some other fashion."

"I could," she hedged, uncomfortable with the idea of change, "but the fact is I haven't yet found a reason to slow down."

Ethan's curiosity sharpened. "What would it take?"

"I don't know." But that wasn't completely true. Since meeting Ethan she'd started imagining lazy Sunday mornings in bed and endless hours of conversation and great sex. "Maybe the right guy to come along?"

"You don't sound convinced."

Sienna regretted her impulsive answer. "Obviously, it's all just speculation and I won't know how I feel until I find him." For some reason, talking with Ethan about a potential relationship with a nonexistent man was making her anxious. "And that's not likely to happen anytime soon."

"You never know. He might be closer than you think."

Sienna shook her head. "It's a chicken-and-egg thing. I don't have a man in my life encouraging me to slow down and I can't invest time in a relationship unless I slow down."

"Sounds like there are a lot of unhappy men in Manhattan who haven't had the pleasure of your company," he stated, brown eyes dancing with sensual intent. "So if you're not dating, how do you spend your downtime?"

"In bed." When he raised his eyebrows, she clarified. "Sleeping." His disappointment made her insides do funny things. "Or hanging out with my friends."

"What about your family? Do you see much of them?"

"Tegan and I text a lot, but she's busy and my parents…" The way she trailed off was telling and from Ethan's expression, he wanted to ask her more about it. "Let's just say I'm a middle child and that my parents are both more preoccupied with my siblings."

"You make it sound like you feel left out."

Was she imagining things or had he leaned forward as if her answer bore some significance for him? She pondered the family photos on his cousin's Instagram feed. How his dark hair and brown eyes made him stand out among his blond relatives. Did he also feel like an outsider? Yet were their situations at all the same? His family so obviously adored him.

"It's more like I'm different than either of my siblings," Sienna explained. "Aiden is just like my dad. He's super outgoing and knows everybody in town. He's also a bit lazy and can be frustratingly scatterbrained at times. But he's the only boy and firstborn. As far as my parents are concerned, he is the golden one."

"And Teagan?"

"My mother's pride and joy. Beautiful, blonde and built like a model with impeccable fashion sense." *Everything I'm not.* "Around the time Teagan turned thirteen, my mother got the idea to start her own fashion line. Since I love to draw, I contributed some sketches and a couple of them were developed for the first collection. But somehow my mother forgot to give me any credit and when it came time to choose the face of the company, my mother picked Teagan. They've been a wildly successful fashion team ever since and nobody has any idea that I was once involved."

"So you draw?"

"I do." She paused to adjust to the change of topic, relieved to move on from her difficult childhood. With an impish grin, she added, "When I'm inspired."

"What inspires you?"

You do. "Mostly the human form." She'd already mentally undressed him earlier. It couldn't be much naughtier to imagine sketching him in all his naked glory. "My senior thesis was devoted to the human body in all its forms."

"I'd be happy to pose for you." His eyes danced with wicked allure. Could he read her mind? If so, sex with him would be beyond amazing. "If you're feeling inspired, that is."

"Well." She took a sip of wine to ease her suddenly dry mouth. "Point me to the nearest art supply store."

After dinner, Ethan and Sienna strolled historic streets south of Broad through the shadows created by streetlamps and lush landscaping. A light breeze, perfumed by jasmine and roses, offered intermittent relief from the weight of the humid air. Beyond the iron fences and tall brick walls, light spilled through the windows of hundred-year-old mansions, the warm glow guiding their path.

Ethan savored watching Sienna absorb the beauty of the historic district the same way he'd relished each bite of his dinner. He enjoyed the sensual pleasure of hearing her inarticulate delight as some sculpture or architectural feature caught her eye. The brush of her arm against his as her balance shifted while she negotiated a transition in the pavement from concrete to brick.

"You're probably bored to tears," she said as they reached a corner and had to decide whether to keep going straight or turn. "I'm used to the noise and bustle of New York. It's so peaceful here."

"I'm fine to keep going if you are," he answered. "White Point Garden and the Battery are a few more blocks down. The sun has already set so you won't be able to see much, but at least you'll know where it is in case you want to come back during the day."

"I think to save my feet for all the sightseeing to come we should head back." But what she did next surprised him.

A formidable brick wall bordered the sidewalk where they stood. Sienna took a backward step toward it, gliding into the shadows cast by a nearby crepe myrtle. Her fingers caught the sleeve of his linen jacket, the tug so delicate he might have missed it if not for the way her invitation lit up his body. Did she hope he'd press her against the wall, slide his lips over hers and make her moan? Because that's what he wanted to do. Yet, instead of following through on his impulses, he stared at the pattern of her bright dress against the dull red-gray bricks, all the while wondering what the hell was stopping him.

"I wouldn't want you to end up with blisters from too much walking," he said, trying to sort out if she needed a moment to rest or if her mind had swerved down the path his had gone.

If he closed the gap between them, would she wrap her arms around his neck and draw him into her space?

"Oh," she breathed, with just the right amount of self-deprecating amusement in her voice to make him smile. "I'm sure you can tell by looking at me that I'm not that fragile."

Ethan moved forward while she was lifting the heavy curtain of hair off her shoulders and neck. Her exposed skin glowed in the contrasting shadows and his mouth went dry.

"I will say, though," she continued as he took another step toward her and placed his palm on the bricks beside her head. "Next to you I feel positively delicate."

"You are. You have a delicate nose and chin." He traced each with the tip of his finger. "Delicate bone structure. Delicate hands and delicate feet." He lifted his free hand and placed his palm against hers, demonstrating their different sizes.

She rasped her nails along the light stubble just below his jawline and his breath hitched. A lightning bolt of hunger shot through him. Dismay followed. This was supposed to be his game. His pursuit. She wasn't supposed to arouse him with a single touch. He was in charge of the seduction, of enticing her into surrendering her secrets and her gorgeous body.

Yet Ethan found himself threading his finger into her luxuriant waves and savoring the silky slide of the soft strands against his skin. He half closed his eyes and watched her expression transform from bold curiosity to wary anticipation. The war between her uncertainty and longing confused him. What could make her afraid to want him? And which emotion would rule the day?

He had a solid plan to find out.

Or he did until she ran playful fingers through his hair.

"Thanks for the fun night." Her soft breath puffed against his cheek before she kissed him there, a warm peck that gave him a quick sample of her soft, full breasts pressed against his chest and left him aching for more.

It was a friendship buss, he realized, barely holding back a tormented groan. Worse, he no longer knew if she was playing him or if her sweetness was honest and legitimate. He searched her eyes for the flicker he'd seen over dinner, the one that matched the fire building beneath his skin. For one breathtaking second he saw what he'd been looking for. That moment was all he needed to take her hand in his and lift the inside of her wrist to his lips.

"It was my pleasure," he responded, thrilling to the gasp that escaped her.

The irregular rise and fall of her chest was creating chaos inside him. He was dying to have those soft breasts squashed against him. To peel off her clothes and expose their perfect contours to his eyes, hands and mouth.

"No, really," she murmured, "the pleasure was all mine."

He dove into her gaze, saw her eagerness and her vulnerability. She wanted him. The discovery didn't fill him with triumph so much as wonder. All his suspicions and scheming fell away. When it came to this woman, this moment, he wanted nothing to get between them.

"There's more than enough pleasure for us both."

Taking her chin, he tipped her face to the perfect angle. Anticipation was eating him alive, but he would only get one shot at a first kiss with her. He intended to make it memorable.

Her startled eyes slid shut as he grazed his lips over hers. The kiss reminded him of jazz. A call and response exchange with bright notes of trumpet, intricate piano improvisation and beneath it all a heartbeat thrum of bass.

Ethan wrapped his arm around her waist and slowly brought her snug against him. This was everything he'd craved, but so much more. The world slowed, compressed, faded. Images of the future flashed in his mind. Bare skin. Soft moans. Greedy hands. Feverish lips. The sharp nip of her teeth. The hot, snug grip of her around his erection.

Sienna melted in his arms, her lush curves pliant against him. Releasing her chin, he feathered the tips of his fingers down her neck and over her collarbone. His mind fogged as she shivered. In that moment, he knew there was nowhere else he wanted to be. They fit together. Belonged together. It was as if his entire life he'd been moving toward this exact instant. A perfect first kiss with a woman who brought every cell in his body to full awareness.

His skin tingled where her fingertips explored. Along his cheekbone, around the rim of his ear, down his neck and around to his nape. Letting the embrace slowly build was both torment and pleasure. He trailed his tongue along the seam of her lips, knowing she'd open for him. Satisfaction exploded when she did. Their breath mingled. She tasted of the raspberry-and-dark-chocolate dessert they'd shared.

The blare of a car alarm hit them both like an ice bath after a muscle-loosening sensual massage. Sienna responded by jerking free of the kiss. Silently cursing the untimely interruption, Ethan tightened his fingers for the briefest of seconds until he registered the tensing of her muscles and let go.

Her gaze darted about as if searching their surroundings for a place to hide. When the empty street offered no protection, she fluffed her hair, gave a nervous laugh and retreated a step. Ethan ground his teeth and acknowledged that the sexy mood was shattered.

"I guess I should take you back to my grandfather's house." While it was the courteous offer to make, he was counting on her to suggest a different destination entirely. In fact, he was on the verge of inviting her back to his place when she nodded.

"It's getting late," she agreed, "and I have a 6:00 a.m. call with an art dealer in Paris."

"Aren't you supposed to be on vacation?" He offered his arm to her before turning back the way they'd come."

Sienna's fingers closed around his biceps. "I have a hard time doing nothing."

He felt a wolfish smile form, thinking of all the ways he could keep her entertained. "If you like to keep busy then I'm the guy for you."

"You don't say." She sounded slightly breathless. "What did you have in mind?"

"Have dinner with me again tomorrow," he suggested, shooting a friendly leer her way. "And I'll show you."

Five

The morning after her dinner with Ethan, Sienna headed to the Gibbes Museum of Art on Meeting Street in Charleston's historic district. Housed in a beaux arts building since 1905, the museum had a collection of ten thousand works of fine art with many connected to Charleston or the South. She'd been particularly eager to study the depiction of the city's complicated past, from the highs of wealth and culture to the lows of slavery and war.

When she'd announced her plans the day before, several of Teagan's family members had offered to accompany her to the museum. Knowing that her measured pace viewing the exhibits would frustrate any companion, she'd turned them all down. For Sienna, art wasn't just a commodity that her clients invested in, but an opportunity to see inside someone's heart, mind and soul and experience what they were feeling. She loved that moment when she gazed at a painting and found her mind opening to another's point of view.

With so much to absorb, Sienna planned to spend the entire day at the museum. Her last stop before breaking for lunch was the observation windows that allowed visitors a behind-the-scenes look of the work of curators and conservators. Her best friend, Gia, was a conservator for the Guggenheim back in New York and Sienna found the work fascinating.

After picking up a salad at the museum's coffee shop, Sienna wandered through the classically landscaped Lenhardt Garden. Then it was back inside to view the exhibition of twentieth-century American regionalism and the Charleston Renaissance that spanned thirty years beginning in 1915.

She was admiring the innovative display of three hundred miniature portraits when her senses were assailed by a familiar masculine scent. Glancing to the side, she spied Ethan an instant before he wrapped a strong arm around her waist and brushed his firm lips over her temple. Although the casual display of affection jangled her nerves, she relaxed against his side and savored the latent power of his hard body. In her world people greeted each other with fake smiles and air kisses. The demonstrative familiarity from Ethan and his cousins was slowly dissolving her usual reserve.

"You look fantastic," he said, the compliment slipping easily from his lips.

Today, she was wearing another outfit purchased during her shopping expedition with Teagan and her cousins. Sienna felt feminine and comfortable in the loose-fitting maxi dress, though with a print of pink watercolor poppies on a black background, it was a bold choice for her.

"Thanks." She found herself blushing for no good reason except that his hungry gaze hit the accelerator on her sexual drive. "You do, too."

He was casually dressed in khakis and a blue-and-white-striped button-down open at the neck and with the sleeves rolled up to expose his muscular forearms. Honestly, the man could wear a parka and a ski mask and his massive amounts of sex appeal would still be overwhelming.

"Have you enjoyed the museum?" Ethan asked.

"Yes," Sienna replied in a breathless rush, delighted by his unscheduled appearance. "It's quite wonderful." She glanced at her watch and saw that it was nearly three o'clock. "What are you doing here?"

"I thought it might be fun to see the museum through your eyes so I canceled my afternoon meetings and skipped out early."

"I'm so glad you did, but are you sure it's okay to do that?" She imagined Teagan's glee at finding out that Ethan was shirking his duties.

"If you don't want me here…" Disappointment shadowed his eyes as he trailed off, misinterpreting her question.

"Oh, no!" she exclaimed, reaching for his arm, eager to reassure him that his company was welcome. "It's not that. I was thinking this might not be the most exciting afternoon for you. I've been known to lose track of time while staring at a painting."

"If I get bored, I'll just stare at you." He took her hand and brushed a kiss over her knuckles.

At the touch of his lips, she let loose a disconcerted chuckle. She scanned his expression, searching for mockery. "I definitely won't be able to concentrate if you do that."

A smug smile came and went as he turned to the display case before them. "What are you looking at here?"

"These are miniatures. Before photography, people had tiny portraits painted of their loved ones. They were tokens of affection they could keep close to their hearts. Some of them were worn as jewelry." She pointed to a two-inch-high oval frame of pearls and rubies that encased an enamel-on-porcelain painting of a gentleman. "Some of them were exchanged between courting couples." She indicated two miniatures that had been painted in 1801. "These would've been worn on a chain and might've included some ornamental hairwork or a romantic inscription."

When she glanced over to see if she'd succeeded in boring Ethan to tears, she caught him eyeing her in bemusement. She hid her relief behind a wry smile.

"Now you see why I usually come alone to a museum. I find all this stuff far too fascinating for the average person."

"You really are passionate about all this, aren't you?"

"You sound surprised."

A fond glow lit his brown eyes. "I guess it's because you keep surprising me."

His response struck all the right notes. Sienna slipped her hand around his biceps and almost purred at the power surging beneath her fingers. Her stomach fluttered as her mind recalled the kiss the night before. Would there be a repeat today? She was feeling needy enough to make sure it did.

"I feel the same way," she admitted, and then experiencing that same click of connection she'd noticed the night before, Sienna beamed at him. "In fact every moment in your company is wonderful."

When he didn't respond right away, she worried that she'd freaked out the elusive bachelor. She was scrambling for a way to gracefully backpedal when he stopped walking and before she knew what hit her, he'd wrapped his arm around her waist and spun her into a romantic dip.

There, in the middle of the museum, Ethan tangled his fingers in her hair and dropped a lingering kiss on her lips. She threw herself into the embrace, as deliriously happy as any heroine in a rom-com, letting herself be swept up in the sizzle of his kisses and the excitement of being so sweetly manhandled. By the time he broke the kiss, she was breathless, light-headed and tingling all over.

"I think it goes without saying," he murmured, his gaze sliding over her bright cheeks and parted lips, "that I find your company pretty wonderful, as well."

"You do have a knack for saying the perfect thing to get a girl's heart fluttering," she bantered back, uncharacteristically giddy as he maintained his snug hold on her for several seconds before whirling her back to a full upright position.

Swaying on her feet, Sienna commanded her foolish heart to settle down as he made a show of reluctance before releasing her. She blew out a quiet breath as they moved arm in arm toward the next exhibit. Thank goodness she wasn't going to remain in Charleston much longer. Knowing this interlude had an expiration date allowed her to experience something she'd never felt before without fear that she'd end up brokenhearted.

An hour later, they exited the museum and emerged onto Meeting Street. Squinting at the bright sunlight, Sienna paused on the checkerboard walkway that led from the entrance to the street and dipped into her purse for her sunglasses.

Thus armored, she glanced Ethan's direction. "Where to?"

"I'd planned for us to go out on my family's boat and then have a quiet dinner."

She picked up the past tense. "If something came up, I understand. We can try another time."

His eyebrows lifted at her quick response. "Are you trying to get rid of me?"

"Oh, no. Of course not."

"Good. Remember when I said that I'm generally the only one who uses the family boat? Well, Poppy sent me a text and invited us to go out on it with her friends."

Ethan appeared displeased at the turn of events and Sienna wondered how many of his past conquests could be counted amongst his cousin's friends. Was he worried if she met them that the stories she might hear would scare her off? If so, it was rather charming that he cared about her opinion of him.

"So," he continued, "we can either go with them or skip the harbor tour and find something else to do before dinner."

Her skin flushed as she imagined all the things they could do to kill the time. "I'm okay with whatever you want to do."

Sliding his gaze over her hot cheeks, he smiled. "Let's head over to the boat. Poppy indicated they won't arrive for a while yet. We can have it all to ourselves for the time being."

Knowing exactly what was on his mind, Sienna found herself tongue-tied and dry mouthed as they headed to the marina on the Ashley River, not far from his grandfather's estate. The boat was an immaculately maintained forty-five-foot cruiser complete with a kitchen above and two staterooms with adjoining heads below, and an indoor/outdoor lounge area. Sienna recalled the way Ethan had lit up when discussing being on the water and noticed how he grew instantly relaxed as soon as they stepped aboard.

"This is quite a party boat," Sienna exclaimed, noting the swim platform off the back, seating for six inside the cockpit and room for another eight on the back deck.

"It's seen its share of good times," Ethan murmured cryptically, indicating the stairs that led below.

"I imagine."

Ethan peeled off his coat and shoes before depositing them in a closet located in the large aft cabin. While he rolled up his sleeves, Sienna kicked off her sandals and tucked them and her purse into the same cabinet. Then, they faced each other in the snug space and their eyes met.

A delicious thrill rushed though Sienna. "When did you say your cousin and her friends were coming by?" Her gaze flicked to the bed a few short feet away.

"Sometime around five." He stepped closer and caressed her arm.

Tiny hairs lifted as his touch passed over them and she shivered. When his hand neared hers, she spread her fingers and he slid his between them. A zap of sensation flashed through her body and she gasped.

"That's almost an hour away." As anticipation zoomed through her, Sienna struggled to breathe. "What are we going to do to fill the time?"

He slid his hand beneath her hair, playing with a loose curl before cupping her nape. "We could start with a cocktail?"

"We could…" The slow buildup of hunger was both torment and pleasure. The ache between her thighs needed relief, but she was loving the hazy rise of passion too much to rush.

His thumb brushed her cheek. "Or…"

"Yes?" She set her hand over his, ready to guide him to where she burned.

"I have a couple other ideas."

Suspecting they would be far more intoxicating than alcohol, she purred, "Do tell."

"How about I show you instead?"

He took her by the shoulders and turned her until she faced away from him. Her nerve endings prickled with delight as he shifted the heavy drape of her hair aside and trailed his hot breath along her neck.

"You smell so good," he murmured, dipping his nose into the sensitive skin beneath her ear.

"Oh," she blurted out in a breathless moan, moisture breaking out on her skin as his tongue flicked the underside of her ear.

"Oh?" he echoed, his wicked laugh making her nipples tighten and her stomach muscles clench.

"Oh."

A throaty half chuckle, half cry tore free from her as he caged her body against his with a palm over her ribs just below her breasts. Although she couldn't have summoned the strength to escape his embrace even if she'd been inclined, she could only quiver and pant as he drove her crazy. He nuzzled and nipped down her neck and along her shoulders. The combination of soft lips and rough stubble caused her intimate muscles to contract.

"Sienna." He whispered her name and she melted, her bones liquifying as he skimmed his fingertips over her abdomen and hesitated just below her belly button.

"Yes, Ethan?"

He traced the top edge of her panties through the fabric of her dress. "Can I touch you?"

"Yes." Her voice, stripped bare and raw, broke as his fingers slid toward her mound. "Please."

A whimper built in her throat when he shifted di-

rection and coasted his hand over her hip and down
her leg. At the rate he was moving, it would take forever before he located the hem of her dress. To aid him,
she grabbed handfuls of the silky material, lifting the
long skirt and baring her thighs to his questing touch.
She sucked in one wildly erratic breath after another
as she waited for him to reach the impatient throbbing
between her thighs.

"Ethan." Reaching back, she gripped his thigh and
rotated her hips, rocking against the bulge hardening
below his belt.

"Sweet mercy, woman," he growled.

"Touch me," she rumbled back between clenched
teeth, the depth of her lust fueling her desperation.

"Easy."

But chaotic cravings tormented her. For a second
she thought he might be inclined to tease her further
and she was about to go into more detail where she so
badly wanted his hands, but then the pads of his fingers drifted past the raised hem and stroked the front
of her panties, grazing her clit through the fragile barrier. Pleasure detonated in her belly, ripping a startled
cry from her, followed by a long moan. She quaked
and shuddered as he touched her in the exact same spot
again before venturing lower.

"Holy sh…" he hissed as he feathered the panel
above her core. "You are so wet."

"Do that again. Only more." She was unconcerned
that she was begging. "Please."

Ethan dipped beneath the elastic of her waistband
and slipped over her folds. "How's this?"

"Good."

"Good?" His husky tone caressed her senses even as his long fingers slanted into her wetness, spreading the moisture over her clit over and over, circling it in relentless, intoxicating strokes. "Let's see if we can't do better."

Craving his invasion, she widened her stance, opening herself up. He teased her entrance, before gently easing a finger inside. Her breath stopped as he touched a particular spot inside her. Her vision went black for a second as pleasure rocked her.

"Oh…"

"You like that?" The husky question brought her back to the cabin and the wonderful play of his finger as it moved in and out of her.

Dizzy with pleasure, she rocked her hips and he increased the pace to match. Her legs trembled as her skin burned. Too hot. Too reckless. She needed…to… come…

Sweat broke out on her forehead as her climax began building. She strained toward the goal, barely aware that she'd thrown her head back against Ethan's shoulder and there were wild sounds erupting from her throat.

"Come for me," he crooned, fingering her faster, deeper, driving her toward a powerful orgasm. "Let it go."

And then she became unhinged. As she gasped for a breath that would never come, her hips bucked and twitched. She ground herself against Ethan's hand and felt the pleasure tearing loose inside her. She was poised on the edge.

"Sienna."

It was her name on his lips and the tortured breath he sucked in that pushed her into an electric orgasm. Twisting her face toward him, she closed her eyes and focused on the fire burning up through her core and spreading to every cell in her body. Lightning flashed behind her eyelids as Ethan's mouth closed over hers, his tongue plunging deep inside as she climaxed like never before.

Aftershocks continued to rock Sienna as her consciousness resettled into her body. Grounded once more, she realized Ethan's arm around her waist was the only thing keeping her on her feet. A lusty chuckle gusted out of her.

"Wow." She turned in the circle of his arms and slid her arms around his neck. "That was amazing."

She was just about to plant her lips against his and begin round two when the muffled thumps of footsteps sounded above her head.

"Damn." Ethan settled his forehead against hers with an unhappy groan that echoed the frustration raging in Sienna. As lively voices filtered down from the deck, he gave her a brief kiss that was filled with promise before he stepped back and raked his fingers through his hair. Shooting her a sidelong glance, he murmured, "To be continued."

Ethan gestured for Sienna to precede him from the cabin, giving him a much-needed couple of seconds to recover from the explosive moment he'd just shared with her. As far as revelations went, the most obvious one was that despite her appearance of reserve when it came to sex, she turned it on faster than any woman he'd ever known. He was all the more eager to get her into bed. In fact, the urge to blow off this impromptu party with his cousin and her friends and take Sienna back to his house immediately was strong as he reached the top step and stopped just behind Sienna, reluctant to join the chaos of six chattering women all trying to fix drinks and organize the food they'd brought.

He curved his hand over Sienna's waist, noticing a slight buzz of energy at the contact as he leaned down to murmur, "If you don't want to stay, we could make some excuse and get out of here."

Relief flashed on her face. "Could we?" She smiled uncertainly as she gazed toward the animated women. "It wouldn't be rude to just take off?"

"I'm not sure they'd notice," he murmured, grazing his fingertips up her bare arm and along her shoulder blades to the nape of her neck, smiling when she shivered. Damn, the woman was sensitive. "And I'd really like to continue what we started earlier."

"So would I," she purred.

He hadn't pegged her as a woman who would sleep with a guy on the second date. Date? Is that what they were doing? Damn. He'd sure been behaving more like he had a romantic interest in Sienna than he was spending time with her to ferret out whatever information he could about her sister's plans for his family.

"We need some sort of an excuse for why we have to go," he said, reaching for his phone.

Several new emails had come in since he'd last

looked and his blood froze as it had often since the first message about Teagan from his anonymous friend. Relief swept through him as cued up his email and saw nothing that immediately worried him, but near the bottom was one from a sender he hadn't been expecting.

Ethan had to give the address a hard look before he realized what he was seeing. A preternatural calm came over him as his attention shifted from the email address of the genetic testing service they'd used to find Teagan to the subject of the message. A match had been found. Worry drove a cold spike into his gut. Had the service made a mistake or was it possible they'd found another child of Ava Watts?

He cursed.

Sienna glanced over her shoulder at him. "Is something wrong?" She covered his hand where it rested on her waist and the warm pressure grounded him.

Ethan shook his head to clear it. "I'm not sure," he muttered, keeping his voice low to avoid being overheard. And then for good measure, he brought his lips close to her ear and added, "I got an email from the genetic testing service."

The women's voices fell away as Sienna turned around and fixed him with her gaze. Their lips were so close, the tiniest movement would put her mouth in contact with his. He could lose himself in the lush softness of her lips and forget about the damn email for at least a little while.

"Something having to do with Teagan?"

"I don't know. Let me check."

Ethan opened the email and read the message. His heart stopped. He reread the words. A curse slipped from his lips as their implication washed over him.

"Ethan?" Sienna's hand curved over his thigh, sending his nerve endings into overdrive. "Is something wrong?"

Her voice sounded as if it came from a long way off. Blood roared in his ears. He read the message again as if doing so might change the words and alter the meaning.

"Are you okay?"

"No." He had no idea what question he was answering. "I mean, yes, I'm okay. Everything's fine."

He looked up and found Sienna's blue-gray eyes fastened on him. The concern he read there caught him off guard. She didn't know him. How could she possibly be concerned about him? And yet there it was.

"It's just… I really need to get out of here," he said. "I'll go get our stuff and meet you on the dock."

To his relief, she merely nodded and began moving toward the women. Ethan's heart was pumping madly as he grabbed their shoes and walked through the group, adding his excuses to Sienna's as he went.

"Where are you going?" Poppy demanded as he bid her goodbye and kissed her cheek.

"This party is a little too rowdy." Ethan lacked the wits to come up with a better excuse.

Poppy regarded him dubiously. "You usually like being the only guy surrounded by a pack of beautiful women." Poppy's gaze went past him to where Sienna waited. "Or maybe it's just one beautiful woman you're interested in these days."

"Ah…" Damn, what did he say?

Poppy leaned in and murmured, "We all think she's great."

Ethan forced a smile. He lacked the time or the inclination to explain that his interest in Sienna was in part to keep an eye on what she and Teagan were up to regarding the CEO position at Watts Shipping. That was his problem and for now, he didn't want it to influence how any of the other members of his family viewed Teagan.

He gave a short nod. "That she is."

Arriving beside Sienna on the dock, he handed over her sandals and purse. While she slipped into her shoes, he took a few seconds to clamp down his expression and gather his scattered emotions.

"Okay, what's going on?" Sienna demanded when he took her hand and began to move along the dock. "You seem really freaked out."

"The service found a match." He exhaled, surprised how shaky he felt. "For me. A family member wants to make contact. If I agree, the testing service will make our email addresses available to each other."

Through his daze, Ethan noticed Sienna scrutinizing his expression and immediately wondered if he'd just made a huge mistake. No doubt she was already dying to run to Teagan with the information so they could plot how best to use it to oust him from Watts Shipping.

"That's good news, right?" she said, nothing but concern in her voice.

"I guess." He met her gaze, fearing his stark confusion was on full display. "I didn't see this coming."

"But you took a test. Didn't you think you'd make a connection?"

"It's been months. I didn't imagine that I'd connect with anyone." He paused, letting that sink in for a moment, before finishing, "After all this time."

"I get it." And no doubt she did, having experienced her sister's recent discovery about her connection to the Watts family. "Teagan had been in the database for almost two years before she found you guys."

Sienna squeezed Ethan's hand. Her show of solicitude appeared genuine and part of him welcomed her comfort. But a stronger impulse warned him to reject her reassurance. He couldn't appear weak. When he stiffened, Sienna frowned, but maintained her firm hold. Her solace pained him. How could he accept her help when he didn't trust her?

"Sorry," he murmured. "It's a lot to take in."

And he wasn't accustomed to sharing his true self with anyone. Much less exposing his innermost fears to someone he shouldn't trust.

"Of course it is." Her gaze softened. "I imagine your head is spinning right now."

He forced his lips into a smile, resenting her compassion even as it warmed him. "It is."

"If you need a sympathetic ear to hear you out, I have some idea what you're going through."

They'd only just met, yet she obviously hoped he'd bare his soul to her. That was brazen of her. Why didn't she assume he'd save his confidences for his family?

Yet when he considered how upset his mother and father would be when they discovered he'd been searching for his blood relatives, Ethan realized that having a neutral person to talk to might be helpful. Not that Sienna was a disinterested party. He needed to worry what she'd share with Teagan.

"Maybe tomorrow," he heard himself saying, troubled by the temptation to confide in her. "I need some time to wrap my head around things."

"Whenever you're ready, I'll be there for you."

Ethan blew out his breath as emotions buffeted him. "You know," he began slowly, measuring his words. "I never thought about how this must've been for Teagan. Or maybe I didn't want to think about it."

Sienna paused before answering, as if carefully preparing her response. "It's been a roller coaster of a few months," she admitted. "I think it's the fear of the unknown that worried her so much in the beginning."

"That was a concern for our family, as well. You know about Lia's and my role in that." Guilt flashed through him. He rubbed his eyes. "It caused a lot of confusion and no small amount of heartache when the truth came out. And then we found out about Teagan." He heaved a sigh. "Once the initial proof determined she was Ava's daughter, our family was excited that we'd found her at last, but wary, as well."

"Your mother said you'd been searching for her for a long time."

"Years and years. I don't know why it hadn't occurred to us to try a genetic testing service sooner."

"Maybe you didn't expect that Teagan would be looking for you in return."

"Why was she looking?"

"After our father made it clear that he wanted our brother to run Burns Properties, Teagan became determined to find her biological family. I think it was the first time she got a taste of what it felt to be snubbed." She covered her mouth, eyes widening as if regretting the disloyal remark. "It was a stressful journey for her, but I know she's really happy to find you all."

"It's been good for us." Beneath his lighthearted response was a deep well of melancholy he'd kept hidden. "Being able to bring her back to the family has given my grandfather a great deal of peace."

"It's none of my business and you don't have to tell me if you don't want to, but what prompted you to look for your biological family?"

"You mean after all this time? Why now?"

Sienna nodded. "Was it because your family was so determined to find your missing cousin?"

"I guess seeing the happy ending that we got with Teagan made me think my own could be just as good."

"But now you're not sure?"

"It's definitely a step into the unknown." He was shocked by the acute fear twisting in his gut. It was clear that he'd assumed the genetic testing service was a long shot and hadn't prepared for the potential heartache of learning the reasons he'd been rejected by his birth mother.

And was he afraid of who she might be? In Teagan's case, she'd been adopted by one of Manhattan's

wealthiest and most influential families and found out
her birth family was equally powerful in Charleston.
How would she have felt if she'd been the daughter
of a couple of nobodies who could cause her embar-
rassment? Teagan's businesses thrived because of her
public image. Negative publicity from some deadbeat
relatives could become problematic.

Ethan might not have those same concerns, but he
did have a lot of money. If his birth family wasn't well
off, meeting Ethan might be akin to finding out they
had a relative who'd won the lottery. They might all
descend on him with their hands out.

"As for why I started looking," he continued, "it's
like I'm out of sync with the rest of my family. Nothing concrete has happened and I can't point to what
prompted me to feel as if I don't belong."

This time when Sienna attempted to soothe him, he
didn't resist. In fact, he was thinking the best way to
escape the heavy emotions weighing him down would
be to re-create the moment earlier when she'd come
hard and fast beneath his touch.

"I would never claim to understand the emotions
an adopted child or adult might experience," she said,
her blue-gray eyes the quiet sea after a storm. "But I'm
not a stranger to feeling like an ugly duckling among
a family of swans."

"Something else that's been bothering me since sub-
mitting the test," Ethan said, "is what if they weren't
looking for me? What if it was just some random test
that they took because they were curious about their

genealogy? What if they had no idea that they were going to connect with someone?"

"You won't know until you contact them," Sienna said. "But I'm sure no matter what caused them to be in the database, they can't be anything but thrilled to welcome you into their family."

In any case, the genie was well and truly out of the bottle. And instead of clamping down on his inner turmoil and presenting a confident facade to Sienna, he'd given her a significant glimpse of his fear.

"I hope you're right."

Six

Sienna was a little surprised when Ethan insisted on taking her to dinner in the aftermath of learning he was on the verge of connecting with his birth relatives. He took her to the Peninsula Grill where they sat across from each other in a cozy booth beside a hand-painted mural of a low-country rice harvest, sipped coconut cake martinis and ate oyster stew with mushrooms and grits.

Although he seemed mostly present as they chatted about southern cooking, Charleston's history and Sienna's plans to visit the Old Slave Mart Museum the following day, Sienna could tell his attention wavered numerous times during the meal. So, after vacillating between the restaurant's famous coconut cake and key lime pie, finally settling on the latter, Sienna decided to address the elephant in the room.

"I know earlier we talked about continuing our evening in a more private setting," she began, heat flooding her cheeks as she replayed their sexy encounter on the boat. "But I think you've got a lot on your mind and I should probably head back to the estate."

"I do and you deserve nothing less than my full attention."

Despite her disappointment with how the evening was ending, Sienna's lips twitched into a half smile when he took her hand as they exited the restaurant. After their companionable conversation over dinner, both Ethan and Sienna were silent during the short drive back to his grandfather's home.

For her part, Sienna was keenly aware of his strength and temptingly masculine scent. As they neared the estate, she was on the verge of saying to hell with her earlier decision and begging him to find them a quiet spot to make out when they reached the driveway and the chance slipped away.

Gallant as always, Ethan walked her up the stairs to the front door and punched in the code that unlocked it. Sienna hesitated before entering, her nerves popping and zinging as she wondered if he'd kiss her good-night.

"I'm really glad you came to Charleston," he said, his heartfelt tone surprising her.

Her stomach fluttered. "You are such a charmer," she said, retreating into flirty banter.

"I mean it."

She gave an awkward chuckle. "I'd better go in before I say something foolish and awkward." She'd hoped her teasing would summon one of his heart-stopping smiles, and there it was.

"Like what?"

A breeze caught her hair, blowing strands across her face. With her expression concealed, she summoned the courage to speak her heart. "I like you."

"I like you, too." Ethan swept her hair behind her ears, and then cupped her face. "A whole lot."

Sienna counseled herself not to overthink it as his lips claimed hers in a kiss of such directness and determined passion that her whole body came to life. She moaned as her muscles melted, but before things escalated too far, he broke off the kiss.

"Thanks for dinner," she murmured, setting her hand on the door handle. "And if you want to talk about what came up today…let me know."

"About that," Ethan began, a frown appearing. "Can you not mention that I might've found my birth family?"

"Of course." She was a little shocked that he believed she'd share such an intimate and personal revelation. On the other hand, given his close-knit family, no doubt they had trouble keeping things from each other. "I wouldn't dream of telling anyone."

Sienna was in a thoughtful mood as she trudged up the stairs to her room on the third floor. As she replayed all that had happened in the last few hours, her mind and body tugged her attention in opposite directions. She couldn't settle on what to process first. Although Ethan's discovery about his birth family was by far the safer topic for her to ponder, that incredible kiss on the boat continued to reverberate through her body, filling her with anxiety and eagerness.

The strong attraction between them promised the sex would be fantastic, but with everything he now had going on, she was left to wonder if they'd go out again. And when that happened, how she could make sure next time they'd end up at his house alone?

Suddenly, she was imagining her hands sliding over Ethan's broad chest, her lips gliding down the strong column of his throat. Would he groan when she played with his nipples? Lose his mind when she wrapped her lips around his erection?

"You're home early."

Caught up in her lusty thoughts, Sienna yelped when she entered her room, not realizing Teagan had come up behind her. Her sister crossed to the love seat beneath the window and sprawled on it. Disappointment flooded Sienna. She'd been looking forward to some time alone to relax and fantasize about Ethan. With her sister curiously regarding her, Sienna slammed the door on her emotions lest Teagan figure out a way to use them to her advantage.

"What are you doing up here?" Sienna asked, dropping her clutch onto the bed and kicking off her heels.

"Looking for you." Teagan swung her feet off the love seat and patted the empty space beside her. "Come tell me all about your dates with Ethan."

Sienna's blood froze. "They weren't dates."

"So we did all this for nothing?" Teagan said skeptically, pointing her finger at Sienna and tracing random squiggles in the air to indicate the makeover. "Tell me, does he like your new look?"

"I guess." Her heartbeat sped up as she recalled his long, slow perusal of her new dress and the way his attention had lingered over her legs, cleavage and lips.

"You guess." Teagan's drawl said she wasn't fooled by her sister's stab at indifference. "Is that why you're turning red? Because you only guess he liked your new look?" When Sienna just stared at her, Teagan gave a throaty laugh. "As for it not being a date, let's talk about that, shall we? You went out for dinner."

"Yes, but he was just being friendly since you were going out with the twins."

Teagan arched an eyebrow. "It's nearly eleven. I'm sure you haven't been eating all this time. So, what did you do after dinner?"

"We talked a bit. He took me for a walk down to the waterfront. The city is just as beautiful at night as it is during the day."

"And did he kiss you?"

Sienna rolled her eyes as if this was a ridiculous question, but saw from her sister's broadening grin that Teagan wasn't fooled.

"From your blush I'd say he did kiss you. Did it curl your toes? Or did you do one of those rom-com foot lifts?"

When Siena stared blankly at her sister, Teagan leaped to her feet and pantomimed lifting one foot off the ground while her arms were wrapped around an invisible lover.

Had she? To be fair it was possible. Her whole body stopped behaving rationally the instant his lips touched hers. As for curling her toes... There was no question in her mind that his kisses had done many disquieting things to her anatomy.

"Don't be ridiculous."

"You like him." Part glee, part taunt, Teagan's declaration plowed into Sienna like a runaway train.

"He's very nice. And so different from the men I meet in Manhattan." Or anywhere else for that matter. Even before Teagan and the twins had taken her shopping or Poppy had cut and highlighted her hair, Ethan had treated her like a woman he was interested in getting to know better.

"Is it that smooth Southern drawl of his? I'll bet it's persuaded more than a few women to do naughty things." Teagan looked like she was enjoying herself a little too much at her sister's expense. "Or his charming manners that hide the fact that he's a wolf in sheep's clothing?"

These reminders of Ethan's player reputation seemed at odds with Teagan's earlier matchmaking. Did her sister want Sienna and Ethan to get together or not?

"I think it's the fact that he doesn't rush me about anything," Sienna said. "The way he takes his time allows me to relax. But I think the best thing is that he never tries to compete with me. He just let me talk and talk. Nobody does that."

"*You* talked?" Teagan made no effort to hide her surprise. "That's not like you."

It irritated Sienna that her sister assumed her re-serve was part of her nature instead of a reaction to their dynamic. From the moment Teagan had arrived in the Burns household, Sienna had been relegated to the background. Teagan commanded everyone's atten-tion and had no qualms about overshadowing anyone who tried to be noticed.

"Maybe you don't know me as well as you think," Sienna murmured.

"Don't be ridiculous," Teagan declared, all frivolity fading from her manner. "You are an open book to me."

"Really?" Sienna made no effort to hide her scorn. Teagan was far too consumed with her own issues to bother with her sister's complex inner world. "So you know what I've been going through these last few months since you found out you were related to the Wattses?"

"You were happy for me."

Something strong and dark rose up in Sienna, a wave of anger and sadness that shocked her with its intensity. "That was only part of it."

"What else?" Teagan asked, looking completely baffled.

Sienna sucked in a steadying breath and let it out slowly. "I was worried about losing you."

"Why?"

"You'd been obsessed with finding your birth fam-ily for so long, and then you found them." Sienna was conflicted about opening up and telling her sister how much she loved her. What if Teagan brushed aside the confession as if it didn't matter? "You wouldn't need me anymore."

"That would never happen," Teagan assured her, flopping back onto the love seat. "You are my sister. That will never change."

"I know that." But deep in her heart lurked that niggling bit of envy at how quickly Teagan had bonded with her Shaw cousins. The three women didn't just look alike, they were outgoing, shared a love of fashion and enjoyed being social.

"So let's get back to you and Ethan. Are you going to sleep with him?"

"Teagan!" Sienna felt her cheeks heat. Confiding in her sister about Ethan would be extremely foolish. "I like him, but that's as far as it goes."

"Well, if you decide to take it further, know that I am wholeheartedly on your side. You are so serious and I think he'd be good for you." Teagan sounded completely genuine. "And since I'm planning on staying in Charleston, it would be nice to have someone besides me to visit whenever you come back to town."

This reminder that her sister intended on taking Watts Shipping away from Ethan dimmed Sienna's good mood. "Anything between Ethan and me won't survive if you succeed in becoming the CEO at his company."

"One has nothing to do with the other," Teagan said, her dismissal coming fast and hard.

"Don't be so sure. I'm your sister. He'll know I'm on your side." And afterward, win or lose, Sienna doubted he'd want to have anything more to do with her.

Teagan narrowed her eyes as she regarded her sister. "You don't expect me to give up my interest in Watts Shipping because you want to hook up with Ethan?"

"No." Sienna dreaded what Teagan would do if she thought Sienna was standing in the way of her plan. "I'm just being realistic. With what you are trying to do, there will come a time where I can't be loyal to both you and him. And when that day comes, you are my sister. You know where I stand."

The morning after Ethan received the notification from the genetic testing service, he swung by Paul's cybersecurity company on his way to Watts Shipping. After dropping Sienna off at his grandfather's house, he'd sent an affirmative response about connecting to his blood relative through the testing service and learned the person looking for him was his birth mother.

After receiving her name and email address, he'd composed a brief, cautious email and sent it, shocked at how his heart had pounded. While waiting for her response, he'd been unable to sleep. Thoughts swirled and bumped in his mind like koi in an overstocked pond. He'd considered how his mother and father would react. Paul was the only member of his family who knew Ethan was looking for his biological family. He hadn't wanted to upset his parents with the search, knowing that they'd both take it hard. It wasn't that they hadn't been great or that he didn't love them deeply, but lately he'd been hounded by this feeling that a piece of himself was missing.

Maybe it was because in the last ten years his grandfather had grown more and more agitated about his missing granddaughter, spurring Ethan to wonder if someone in his birth family was desperately searching for him. He hadn't anticipated the turmoil of dread and eagerness that would erupt when he discovered they were.

"Sorry to drop by without calling," Ethan said, taking a seat on the couch in Paul's office. He accepted a cup of coffee and scrutinized his brother's face. "Damn. You look really good."

"You say that like it's a bad thing."

"I guess I'm still trying to get used to you looking so relaxed and…happy."

Paul smirked. "Quite a change, isn't it?"

Before Lia had come into his life, Paul had been completely absorbed in his business. Since falling for the free spirit, he'd shifted more responsibility to his staff so he could spend more time with his fiancée. Accustomed as Ethan was to his older brother's serious nature, the way Paul smiled all the time these days, and knowing that Lia was the reason, gave Ethan a great deal of satisfaction. After all, she wouldn't be in Paul's life if Ethan hadn't persuaded her to pretend to be their cousin in the first place.

"Honestly, it's a shock that you're in a good mood all the time."

"It's love. You should give it a try."

Ethan shook his head. "You can't expect me to settle down with one girl when there are so many out there looking for a good time."

"I might've bought your too-many-fish-in-the-sea argument before I met Lia. But from the moment she entered my life, I knew that committing fully to the woman I love is the only way to go."

"I'll take your word for it," Ethan said dryly, concealing a flash of envy at what his brother had found with Lia. "But I didn't come here to talk to you about your love life. There are a couple of things on my mind right now. First off, did you have any luck figuring out who sent the emails about Teagan?"

"No. Whoever it is covered their tracks very well."

"Almost as if they knew that a cybersecurity specialist might be hunting them down," Ethan put in.

"Do you think if we dig deeper into her background, we'll find a lot of people who have it in for her?"

"Probably." Ethan didn't find it strange that a successful New York businesswoman had picked up an enemy or two. But was that all it was? Someone out to make trouble for Teagan?

"So, can we check into some of those people?"

"Already on it." Paul gave his brother a searching look. "But all this is something we could've talked about over the phone. What's your real reason for stopping by?"

"I got a different sort of email yesterday."

"Another warning? Or some kind of threat?"

"Neither." Ethan leaned forward, his forearms resting on his thighs, his fingers intertwined. "I submitted my own genetic material for testing."

Paul sat back, understanding dawning. "You got a hit."

"I got a hit," Ethan echoed. "Last night while I was out to dinner with Sienna. She gave me some things to think about."

"Such as?"

"How my reaching out to my birth family will impact the people who raised me and the brother I love."

"If you're worried that Mom and Dad will feel betrayed that you were curious about where you came from, don't be. The minute we found Teagan we all understood what it's like to fill the hole that's been in our lives." Paul paused and considered his brother's expression. "Plus, it's not as if you're going to find anyone better than us."

Paul's unexpected humor made Ethan grin. "The best thing I ever did was invite Lia into our family. She's had an enormously positive effect on you."

"Typical Ethan," Paul said. "Always taking credit for other people's hard work."

"So, you think Mom and Dad will be okay that I've done this?"

"I think they'll support you in whatever you have to do. You know that."

Ethan nodded. "I'll tell them after my trip to Savannah."

"What's in Savannah?"

"My birth mother."

"What?" Paul breathed, looked uncharacteristically staggered. "You found…"

"Her name is Carolina Gates." His voice faltered on her name. "I'm heading down there Wednesday night to meet her."

Paul was recovering his equilibrium. "I think you should tell Mom and Dad before you go."

"What if it doesn't go well with Carolina? Why upset our parents before I figure out if I intend to have a relationship with her?"

"You always keep a wall up between you and those of us who love you. One of these days you're going to find out what a mistake that is."

"Maybe." Ethan bristled. Paul couldn't stop himself from playing all-knowing older brother. "In the meantime, I was hoping you could do a little research on my birth relatives so I know what I'm getting into."

"Of course." Paul pulled out his phone and quickly typed something into it. "I'm glad you're taking steps to protect yourself."

"You know I'm always careful," Ethan said while in the back of his mind crazed laughter erupted.

Who was he kidding? His behavior had grown more destructive over the last year. From lying to everyone about Lia being Ava's daughter to keeping this enormous secret about his search for his birth relatives from his adoptive family and isolating himself in the process. And of course he was letting himself get far too involved with Sienna when he knew she didn't have his best interest at heart.

"I can clear my schedule if you want company on your trip to Savannah."

"I wouldn't want to take you away from Lia."

"Given the situation, I'm sure she wouldn't mind if I was gone for a few days."

While Ethan didn't want to involve his family, Paul's

offer made Ethan realize that it would be nice to have company, someone he could talk to if things got a little too intense. Last night Sienna had demonstrated she understood what he was going through, having recently experienced a similar situation with her sister.

"Thanks," Ethan said. "But I think I'll ask Sienna to come with me to Savannah."

"Sienna?" Paul's eyes narrowed. "But you barely know her."

"True, but she's already been through this with her sister and it'll be easier to be with someone who isn't emotionally involved."

"I thought you didn't trust her."

How did Ethan explain his increasingly conflicted feelings about Sienna? "Not when it comes to helping her sister take over Watts Shipping, but I think in this instance, she'll be helpful."

And with the two of them alone in Savannah, they could more fully explore the attraction between them. Ethan was looking forward to that as much as meeting his birth mother.

"I guess you know what you're doing," Paul said, sounding like a skeptical older brother.

"If I don't," Ethan began with a dry smile, "it wouldn't be the first time I ended up in over my head." But until things blew up, he intended to have the time of his life.

Seven

Sienna sat on the back terrace, laptop open on the table before her, gaze riveted on the charismatic man heading in her direction along the garden pathway. If her sudden breathlessness was anything to go by, her attraction to him had only grown since last night.

"There you are," he declared, a warm smile drawing her attention to the sensual curve of his lips. "I was looking for you."

She closed her laptop and gestured to the chair beside her. He shook his head and held out his hand.

"Walk with me instead."

Sienna couldn't help the delight that spread through her as she took his hand. When he led her away from the house to the relative privacy of the pool house, she had a pretty good idea of what this was about.

"You got an email from your birth family."

"My birth mother." He pulled a folder out of his briefcase. "This was what Paul was able to find on her."

Sienna stared at the thick file, wondering if the cybersecurity specialist had created similar dossiers on her and Teagan. As soon as the question popped into her mind, she knew the answer. Of course he had. And no doubt Ethan had read both. So, with all his questions about what she did, he'd already known the answers. Sienna felt the tiniest bit betrayed, but pushed the feeling inside. Given the Wattses' wealth, they would've been crazy not to investigate Teagan and her adoptive family.

"Who is she?" she prompted, curiosity getting the better of her.

"Carolina Gates from Savannah, Georgia. Her family owns Gates Multimedia. My mother…" He swallowed hard, Adam's apple bobbing as he grappled with his feelings. "She submitted the DNA test after finding out I was alive."

Sienna gasped. "What? She thought you were dead? How?"

"She didn't go into the details, but it sounds like she was seventeen when she got pregnant with me and it was a complicated birth. Long story short, she thought I died."

Hearing the anguish in Ethan's voice, Sienna gripped his arm. Part of her wanted to lend him support, but mostly she craved a connection with him in this emotionally charged moment.

"How could she not know?"

From his somber expression and the crease between his eyebrows, he was bothered by this same question. "She said she'd explain when we met."

"How did she find out you were alive?"

"There was a nurse who knew that I'd survived. She died recently and left a letter with her lawyer for my mother, explaining what had happened."

The whole situation sounded mysterious and Sienna worried that Ethan might be heading into trouble. "When are you heading to Savannah?"

"I thought I would go down there Wednesday evening and return Sunday. Would you like to come?" This last he said so casually that she thought she'd misheard him.

"I'm not sure I should. This is your first meeting with your biological family."

"It would help if you were there."

His husky-voiced admission made her ache to support him. But it wasn't her place. They barely knew each other. Yet each moment in his company deepened the connection between them. At least on her end. She'd never been in love, but surely this is what it felt like to fall for someone.

"I know it's a lot to ask," Ethan persisted when she didn't give him an immediate answer. "But you've been through this with your sister and since you have so much experience dealing with the whole meeting-the-birth-family thing, I thought maybe you'd understand what I'd be going through."

Although Sienna would never claim to know everything about Ethan after such a short acquaintance, she recognized that asking others for help wasn't something he did easily or at all. Obviously, meeting his birth mother entailed more emotional upheaval than he wanted to go through alone.

"Wouldn't you be better off bringing one of your own family?"

"Honestly, I like the idea of having a neutral party along. I'd be afraid if I asked anyone from my family that they would make it all about them." He caught her gaze and held it. "You haven't done that with Teagan. I could really use your company."

Sienna didn't think he would've asked her without feeling an actual need. She told herself not to be flattered. She was a logical choice given everything he just explained. But the trip might be a good opportunity to see where their connection might lead.

"If you think it would be helpful then I'd be happy to go with you." Sienna paused. "Let me run it past Teagan first. After all, she's the reason I'm here in the first place."

"Of course. I wouldn't want to take you away from your sister. But if you could not mention anything about my birth mother. I haven't figured out what I'm going to tell my parents yet."

"I understand perfectly." Sienna recalled their mother's devastation when Teagan announced that she'd been searching for her blood relatives. "I'll get back to you as soon as I can."

Since Teagan had made plans to go out with the Shaw twins after work, Sienna knew she wouldn't run into her sister at the house and reached out by phone.

"Ethan invited me to go with him to Savannah for a long weekend," she announced when Teagan answered, aware that her voice reflected how excited she was by the prospect. "I thought it sounded like fun."

She expected Teagan to grill her about the trip. But even if Ethan hadn't specifically asked her to keep the reason for the visit secret, Sienna wouldn't have mentioned anything about going to meet his birth mother. This was something Teagan would love to use to stir up turmoil between Ethan and his family.

"He wants to take you out of town," Teagan said, her voice filled with glee. "That's perfect."

Sienna's radar went on full alert. "What do you mean perfect?"

"Just that I know you really like him," Teagan replied, her breezy tone giving nothing away. "And it seems as if he's into you, as well."

"I don't know if that's true," Sienna hastened to assure Teagan. "He invited me along because he thought I might be interested in seeing a little bit more of the South."

The excuse sounded incredibly lame to her own ears, but what did it matter if her sister thought Sienna and Ethan were running away for a romantic few days? Except that Teagan was obsessed with the top position at Watts Shipping and would use any means to sabotage Ethan's chance. Including her sister.

"I think he's interested in seeing a little bit more of you." Teagan's sly glee tainted what could've been a supportive declaration. "And if you can keep him there longer, please feel free. The less time he's around, the more time I have to convince everyone I'm the best one to run the company."

There it was.

Suddenly, Sienna's eagerness to go away with Ethan dimmed. She hated being caught between her sister, whom she loved, and the man she was eager to get to know better.

"You know I hate being a part of your schemes," she said as if stating the obvious would influence her sister's plans.

"What scheme?" Teagan countered. "All I'm looking for is an opportunity to show everyone at the company what I can do without Ethan's years of experience overshadowing me."

Sienna rubbed her temple where a painful hammering kept time with her heartbeat. "Have you been up-front with Ethan about your interest in being the CEO?"

"Why?" Teagan scoffed. "So he can block me at every turn? The direct approach isn't going to work and you know it."

Teagan's determined words warned Sienna that any argument she might make would fall on deaf ears. Her sister had decided on a course of action and she would see it through to its bitter end.

"I still think you should say something to him," Sienna grumbled, aware that she was wasting her breath.

"I'll think about it," Teagan said, her tone saying she'd do no such thing. "Meanwhile, keep him nice and distracted in Savannah for me. And be careful. If he finds out how you feel about him, he'll use that to turn you against me."

"Ethan isn't like that." But even as the hot denial left her lips, she wondered if that was true. How far would he go to secure the CEO position? Was he as ruthless as Teagan? Willing to use any means—anyone—to achieve his goals?

"I've talked to people," Teagan countered. "He's exactly like that."

Knowing it was fruitless to dig for information about her sister's supposed sources, Sienna murmured something noncommittal before ending the call. She sent Ethan a quick text indicating she was free to go, and then turned her attention to what she might take with her. She'd replaced her battered suitcase with a brand-new set of luggage that would accommodate her recently expanded wardrobe.

Sienna opened the armoire and regarded her newly purchased clothes, wondering what she should take. Teagan and the twins had encouraged her to buy things that were perfectly suited for the climate and highlighted her curves. Yet she still felt a little bit like an imposter when she wore them. Teagan believed that fashion made the woman and had been badgering Sienna for years to adopt whatever look was trending.

It wasn't that Sienna couldn't be bothered to shop or spend time becoming a more glamorous version of herself; it was more that she hated being compared to her thinner, beautiful, fashion-forward sister. But was this even an issue anymore? They were no longer in school where every second of every day their peers offered brutal critiques and doled out humiliation.

Buying clothes that flattered her figure and made her feel feminine and happy, followed by seeing Ethan's reaction to her appearance, Sienna knew she'd undergone a fashion revolution. But although she couldn't imagine reverting back to her conservative, well-made suits and monochromatic color palette, she couldn't abandon them altogether.

She selected a couple outfits suitable for meeting Ethan's family and dinners out as well as some more casual things for daytime. After their first moonlight kiss, she'd indulged in some truly luxurious lingerie, and carefully packed every silky item in her new suitcase. She intended to be prepared in case being all alone with Ethan for several days led to something happening between them.

Immediately her body was awash in anticipation, but Sienna took herself in hand. Ethan would be totally focused on meeting his birth mother. The last thing he would be thinking about would be sex with her. Still, she couldn't stop herself from hoping that he'd turn to her if the weekend became emotionally overwhelming. And she planned to welcome him with open arms.

Ethan picked Sienna up at his grandfather's house a little after five. During the two-hour drive from Charleston to Savannah, Sienna watched the landscape flow by and didn't once complain about Ethan's silence. Now, as they neared Savannah, his sense of urgency was transforming into anxiety. Since discovering his birth mother wanted to find him, he'd been focused on meeting her as soon as possible. Now he felt the first inklings of doubt holding him back.

When the sign for the Georgia state line flashed by, Ethan realized he had a death grip on the steering wheel. He flexed his fingers and blew out a long, slow breath.

"Are you okay?"

"For years I thought my mother gave me up, and now I find out she had no idea I was even alive. I didn't acknowledge how angry I was about not being wanted by her until I was notified about the match and now..." He clamped his lips together, recoiling from the wild churn of emotion that swept over him.

The wide expanse of Little Black River appeared ahead of them, its wind-ruffled surface sparkling with early evening sunlight. Bright shards lanced into his eyes, making them water. He blinked rapidly and cleared his vision.

"Now?" she prompted.

"I'm still mad," he went on, "but also relieved. And anxious. There's something troubling in why she thought I was dead and I'm not sure what sort of a situation I'm walking into."

Recognizing his distress, Sienna squeezed his arm in a friendly manner. Her touch galvanized him and without thinking, Ethan reached out and wrapped his fingers around hers. The contact immediately soothed his unease.

"I'm sure she has a lot of story to tell."

He was grateful for her knack for reading his moods

and going with the flow. Just one of several things about her he appreciated. He wondered if she had any idea that during the drive, when he wasn't brooding, he'd been eyeballing the impressive amount of silky leg and cleavage bared by her flirty red-and-white polka-dot wrap dress and pondering how quickly he could get her out of it once they arrived.

"Do you want to stop for dinner before we get to where we're staying?" he asked, a hefty dose of lust lightening his mood. "Or settle in, and then go out?"

"There's a third option," she said, pausing for emphasis. "We could order room service."

He cleared his throat. "Actually, I had my assistant rent us a house, so I'm afraid we're fending for ourselves." He'd been eager to have Sienna all to himself without the awkwardness of public hallways and electronic door locks. "I thought you'd enjoy being in the historic district and as it happens, my birth mother's home is within walking distance."

"I can't wait to explore." Her warm tone gave no hint of reluctance or concern. "Since we'll have a kitchen, why don't we pick up groceries so I can fix us something."

He liked the idea that she wanted to cook for him. The domesticity felt oddly intimate. "That sounds good."

Ethan gave her the address of the house where they were staying and Sienna used her phone to search for the nearest place to buy what they needed. She located a grocery store and began navigating. Her initiative intrigued him. The women he dated expected him to plan and execute everything. In contrast, Sienna demonstrated she was accustomed to doing things on her own. Being with her felt more like a partnership and he enjoyed sharing responsibility with her.

After the grocery stop, they drove through the historic district toward Forsyth Park and their accommodations.

"Did you ever consider coming here for college?" He indicated a sign for Savannah College of Art and Design.

"New York's School of Visual Arts was my first pick, but I actually applied to SCAD as well as several other art schools around the country. SCAD is a great school and what they've done to revitalize Savannah is really impressive, but I am a New York City girl at heart."

Ethan was still pondering her remark as he escorted Sienna up the front walk of the home his assistant had rented for them. He'd been so caught up in the anxiety of meeting his birth mother that he hadn't considered that Sienna would be heading back to New York after their time in Savannah was done. Her leaving meant Teagan would no longer have the advantage of a spy at her disposal. He should've felt relief. Instead, the thought of not seeing Sienna every day filled him with dismay.

Had she told her sister about the reason for their trip to Savannah despite his specific request to keep the matter quiet? It had been a test. If Sienna spilled his secret, he would know exactly what she was made of and that she couldn't be trusted. He had yet to consider what he'd do if she kept his confidence.

"This is a lot of space for just the two of us," she remarked as they entered the expansive foyer, carrying the groceries and their bags.

The rental was a three-thousand-square-foot historic house across from Forsyth Park, a block down from the landmark fountain, one of the most famous sights in Savannah. Given Sienna's love of all things that gave a city its character, he was looking forward to viewing Savannah through her eyes.

"I wanted to make sure you were in the middle of everything."

They found a chef's kitchen at the back of the house and while Sienna put the groceries away, Ethan took their luggage upstairs. Not knowing which of the four bedrooms she'd choose, he left their bags on the landing at the top of the stairs before heading back down. He found Sienna in the living room, perusing one of the guidebooks on Savannah left by the property owner for visitors.

"I did a little reading up before we came." She flashed him a wry smile when he snorted. "And while you're with your family, I will have plenty to keep me occupied."

"About that. I thought maybe you'd come with me to meet my mother. And afterward we can go play tourist." Seeing her surprise at his invitation, he rushed on. "There are a couple graveyards if you're into that as well as several historic buildings and lots to see near the river."

"You didn't come here to sightsee," she reminded him.

"No, but I do so enjoy showing you around."

"Have you spent much time in Savannah?"

Her question awakened him to the fact that he had family here. Family he hadn't known existed until now. Realizing that he had been so close several times in his life to the mother who gave birth to him sent a chill over his skin.

"I've been here a couple times. Once for a wedding and once to apply for an internship during college."

She looked at him in surprise. "An internship? I would've thought that you only worked at Watts Shipping."

"That's basically true. When my older brother followed his passion for computers and started his cyber-security company it naturally fell to me to step into the family business."

She studied him for a long moment. "Was there something else you wanted to do?"

Was she searching for insight to pass along to her sister? Ethan shoved aside his suspicions for the moment.

"Honestly, I never had the chance to consider if I was passionate about pursuing something different."

"Because no one else in your family showed any interest in Watts Shipping?"

"Something like that."

While it was true that he'd toyed with the idea of not working for the family business, in the end, he knew that others were depending on him. The burden of that had sat heavily on his shoulders for most of his twenties. He pondered his fury over Teagan's plans to take Watts Shipping away from him. How ironic that once he'd stopped resisting the future that had been prescribed for him, a challenger would come along and threaten to usurp a job that he wasn't completely sure he wanted.

And now he'd learned that his blood relatives owned a family business of their own. Maybe there was a place for him there. If so, Ethan could stop worrying about Teagan and explore whatever was happening between him and Sienna.

"Shall we go upstairs and figure out where we're going to sleep?"

He hadn't meant for the question to electrify the atmosphere between them, but suddenly he was imagining her beneath him on the bed, naked and eager. The look she shot at him sent blood pounding through his body.

"Ethan."

It was just his name, yet the sound of her voice, half worried, half entreaty, went through him like an electric charge. He slid his arm around her waist, drawing her against him.

"What are we going to do about this?" he asked, dipping his head to nuzzle the sensitive flesh behind her ear.

She shivered as his lips coasted over her skin. "What do you want to do?"

"I'd like to take you upstairs and spend the rest of the night making you come." He cupped her breast, savoring the full curve. "What do you say?"

"I say…let's go."

Her hesitation, slight as it was, caused him to lift his head and stare down at her expression. "If you're not sure, I understand."

"It isn't that I don't want you or this." She pressed her hand over his where it rested on her breast and offered up a slow smile.

"But?" he prompted.

"I just want…" The vulnerability shining in her blue-gray eyes looked entirely genuine. "To be more than a…distraction."

He snorted. "You've been a distraction from the moment you stepped out of the car on that first day." Something her sister had recognized and was probably trying to capitalize on. Ethan tamped down his suspicions and focused on the heat building in his body. "In the best way possible."

"Oh."

Her dazed expression was so enchanting that for a second Ethan wondered if he was wrong to be suspicious. She'd have to be one hell of an actress to affect guilelessness this long without a single slip.

Well, there was one way he could figure her out. Scooping her into his arms, he headed toward the stairs.

Eight

With her stomach in free fall, Sienna wrapped her arms around Ethan's neck and let herself get swept up. They'd been moving toward this moment since he sat down beside her on the front steps of his grandfather's house. Her chest tightened, limiting the amount of air she could pull into her lungs. She knew it was foolish to feel as if she'd known him forever when in fact, they had met less than a week ago. Yet she found herself reading his mind and noticing every shift of emotion that crossed his expression.

He set her down beside the bed and gave the bow of her wrap dress a gentle tug. The garment fell open as the belt came undone, exposing the satin and lace she wore beneath it. He eased the fabric off her shoulders and sent the dress arcing across the room toward the chair in the corner.

Dipping his head, he grazed his lips over her earlobe, and rumbled, "You are so damn gorgeous."

Men had called her beautiful before, but she took their words with a grain of salt. Ethan's compliment sent vivid emotions blazing through her. Her desperate need to believe him made her surrender her power. She could only hope he'd handle her with care.

She began to unbutton his shirt, eager to explore all the muscle rippling beneath his warm skin. While she worked, he popped the buttons on his cuffs so that by the time she slipped the last one free, his shirt just slid off his shoulders and landed on the floor. With both of them breathing a little hard, they stared at each other for several seconds.

"This is happening," she murmured, her heart climbing into her throat.

His eyebrows rose. "If that's what you want."

Was he seriously giving her an out? Sienna had never been more obsessed about having sex with anyone. When it occurred to her he probably didn't feel the same way, she took a half step back. Was she making too much of this moment?

"Of course it is." Suddenly, she was shivering in the air-conditioned space, awash in discomfort as she stood before him in the silk lingerie she'd purchased with him in mind. "Unless you don't want to."

With a husky laugh he eased his palms along the delicate fabric, riding the curve of her hip and indent of her waist. Up and up to the outer curve of her breasts. She'd forgone a bra and his thumbs whisked over her hard nipples, eliciting a low cry.

"I'll always want to."

Always struck her as a definitive word, suggesting something more complicated than scratching a sexual itch. Panic fluttered in the back of her mind like a trapped bird. This was just supposed to be an easy and fun romp before she went back to New York City.

Shutting down her mind, she lifted one hand to his sun-bronzed biceps and flattened her other palm over his heart. "Make love to me, Ethan."

He stroked the thin straps of her slip off her shoulder. The silky fabric caught on her full breasts so she shimmied and wiggled until it reached her hips, baring her torso to his greedy gaze. He ducked his head and grazed his lips over her nipple. Her back arched as he ran his tongue in a circle around the tight bud.

Sienna spread her fingers and sifted them into his thick hair, using the grip to keep her balance as he kissed his way along the slope of one breast and into the valley of her cleavage before making the ascent on the other side. This time, instead of lightly teasing her nipple, he drew it into his mouth, teeth scraping gently against the sensitive flesh, tongue swirling. The suction made her groan with pleasure. The sound transformed into a whimper as he stroked his fingers into the dampness between her thighs, parting her folds so he could tease her entrance.

"You okay?" he murmured, his drawl thick with pleasure as his lips coasted along her neck.

"Good. Great." She gasped, rocking against his hand, feverish to feel him inside her. "More."

"Like this?"

His fingers plunged inside her, catapulting her back to those moments on the boat when he made her come. She arched her back and welcomed his invasion. Tonight there would be no one to interrupt them.

His strokes became a pattern, a slow thrust of his fingers, a sweep around her clit, followed by another deep penetration. Each circuit drove her desire higher, stole all rational thought, made her wild. She clung to his shoulders, writhing against his hand, a shrill keening breaking from her throat as the torture became unrelenting pleasure.

And then the dam burst and the climax hit her. She quaked as wave after wave of ecstasy pummeled her. Electrical charges short-circuited her muscles. Her knees gave way and only Ethan's strong arm around her waist kept her upright. Brushing sexy kisses over her lips, he eased them both toward the bed. As the backs of her legs touched the solid surface, she sat down with an awkward "oof" and released a wild chuckle.

"Are you all right?" he asked, peering down at her.

"I'm better than okay." She set her heels on the mattress and lifted her hips to move her slip from beneath her, snagging her silk panties with her thumb as she did so and sliding everything down her thighs, leaving herself utterly, wantonly naked. "Or I will be when you come here."

* * *

Ethan hadn't spent the entire time ogling Sienna as she'd stripped. After his own pants had hit the floor, he'd stooped to fish out the condom he'd stashed in his pocket. When he straightened and lifted his gaze to find Sienna reclining like some exotic goddess waiting for her human subject to pleasure her, he could do little more than gape.

"Ethan?" She blinked in concern as she looked at him. "Are you okay?"

With the condom clutched between his fingers, he dropped to his knees beside the bed, settled his shoulders between her parted legs and stared at the glorious untamed bush at the apex of her thighs. The women he knew trimmed and waxed to such an extreme that he'd forgotten how glorious their natural beauty could be.

"You are gorgeous," he murmured, trailing his fingers over her. "This is a total turn-on."

"Oh."

"I'm going to make you come again."

With a surprised bark of laughter, which turned into a sharp cry as he ran his tongue through her hot, damp core, Sienna gave herself over to his mastery. Quicker than he imagined possible, she came a second time, harder than the first. As she lay like a rag doll, limp except for the agitated rise and fall of her chest, Ethan shifted onto the bed and covered her with his body. With a smile, he brushed a stray lock of hair away from her face.

"I think making you come is the highlight of my day."

In the grasp of a powerful climax, she'd been absolutely breathtaking. And nothing compared to knowing that he'd been the one to give her pleasure. To drive her into that white-hot orgasm. And she trusted him enough to let go completely.

"How about we see if that's true for me, too?"

She trailed her soft lips along his neck, fanning the fire raging in his veins. Her tongue flicked against the racing pulse in his throat as she slid her fingers over his hip and grazed his erection. The woman was killing him. Half-dizzy from the sensation, he ground his teeth together and fought to keep from erupting like some newbie with his first girlfriend.

Breathing hard, he swooped down and captured her lips, letting lust consume him as he held her round rear end tight in his palms. The throbbing in his shaft grew worse as he slid down to pay homage to her spectacular breasts, enjoying the frantic sounds emanating from her throat.

"No more," she moaned, suddenly levering herself up on her elbows and grabbing the condom he'd left on the mattress beside her. "Put this on. I want you inside me." Her urgent, sexy words made him smile.

"If you're sure…"

"So sure."

His hands weren't all together steady as he sheathed himself. She watched his every move and the light scrape of her fingernails along his thigh drove him to distraction. As soon as he finished, she wrapped her fingers around his erection and the sensation of her strong grip sliding over him made him grit his teeth.

Ethan settled between her thighs. His lips grazed hers. She plunged her tongue forward, stroking deep inside his mouth. A series of deep, drugging kisses followed. Ethan lost himself in their connection, restraining the lust pounding through his veins, wanting to build her pleasure once more to make their joining perfect.

But her frantic gyrations slowly ate away at his willpower. He settled his forearms on either side of her head, raising himself to a plank position over her. He needed to see her face, to reassure himself she was all in. Their eyes met and he saw the desire flickering in her blue-gray depths. With nothing more holding him back, he guided his shaft forward. Positioning himself against her entrance, he nudged the blunt head of his erection against her tight heat.

"Now, Ethan," she gasped, flexing her hips in hungry supplication.

Muscles straining, he eased inside her, feeling her tightness expand to accommodate him. Inch by inch he moved, sliding deeper into heaven.

"This is so good." He needed her to know how amazing she felt.

"Oh, hell yes," she exclaimed, her lashes lifting, fingers digging into his skin.

Finally seated deep inside her, he grazed her lips with his. "I've never needed this more."

"Me neither."

Need roared to life, demanding he move. He pulled back, feeling her inner muscles tighten on him, resisting his withdrawal. Just as smoothly, he thrust into her once more, memorizing her impassioned gasp, knowing it would belong to him forever.

"You like this?" he asked, leaning down to nip at her earlobe.

Her body quaked, muscles clamping down on him once again as he drove into her with more vigorous movements.

"Oh, yes."

"You like how it feels to have me inside you?"

"So much," she panted as he continued to drive into her. "I like it… So, so much."

The sounds she made as he withdrew and pushed forward again made his chest ache. Why did it have to be Sienna he felt this way about? She was everything he'd ever wanted and the timing couldn't be worse. Yet as they strained together toward their fulfilment and Sienna's focus never shifted from his face, Ethan was sure his expression exposed everything he was feeling. But instead of retreating, he let her have it all, showing every emotion from worry to joy to deepest appreciation.

"Oh."

Sienna tensed, her muscles quaking as she squeezed him with fiery, demanding strength. Her gaze snagged his in a soul-stealing connection that turned his world inside out. Her longing ripped him open and made him whole.

Ethan drank in her gasps as she began to come, her body bucking and straining beneath him. As his own pleasure surged, he held on for a brief moment of triumph before she dragged him straight into an explosive, intoxicating orgasm that plunged him into a deep pool of satisfaction.

In the aftermath, he rolled them to their sides and gathered her against him. With their legs tangled, Sienna limp and sated in his arms, her breath a contented purr against his neck, the most astonishing peace claimed him. Ethan nuzzled against her hair and listened to their wild heartbeats sync and slow.

"I think I died and went to heaven," she murmured, lifting her chin so she could peer at him from beneath her long lashes.

A bright bolt of energy lit him up like the midday sun when she smiled. All too aware that her power over him was something that should be freaking him out, Ethan pushed it to the back—way back—of his mind.

"And to think we have the whole weekend ahead of us."

"Not the whole weekend." She placed her palm against his cheek and stroked her fingertips against his forehead and nose. "You are here to meet your mother and spend time with her."

"But we'll be together at night. Here. In this bed."

"Just this bed?" Sienna's gaze flickered toward the window that overlooked the courtyard. "Didn't you say you love the water? There's a secluded courtyard with a pool behind the house."

Amused at where her thoughts had gone, Ethan dipped his head and kissed her with tender passion. "And a bathtub big enough for two up here."

"How's the shower? I've always had a fantasy…"

She trailed off and shot him a wicked grin. "I guess I'll have to show you."

"I guess you will."

As the morning sun filtered through the bedroom windows, Ethan awoke to an empty bed and a flare of panic. Sienna was gone. Anxiety sharpened, waking him more fully. Thrusting up onto one elbow, he rubbed sleep from his eyes and gazed about the room, finding it empty except for Sienna's dress and his pants. His shirt was missing. Above the rapid thump of his heart, the clack of crockery filtered up the stairs and Ethan collapsed back onto the pillows.

His disconcerting response to finding himself alone this morning left Ethan questioning how far his perspective had shifted where Sienna was concerned.

Covering a jaw-cracking yawn with the back of his hand, Ethan slipped from bed and stretched. His stomach growled as the scent of bacon and coffee drifted upstairs. Before seeking out Sienna in the kitchen he fished out his phone and scanned the emails that had appeared in his inbox overnight. Seeing no message from his anonymous source, he breathed a sigh of relief.

Immediately he was disgusted by the level of trust he'd put in some unnamed meddler as opposed to trusting his own instincts. Surely with all the time he'd spent with Sienna, something would've triggered his suspicions by now. And it wasn't as if he'd turned a blind eye because he was attracted to her. For the last week he'd actively been watching for any slip up.

Well, there hadn't been any last night. Not a single qualm had marred their hours of soul sharing and blissful lovemaking. In the aftermath of connecting physically with her, he'd felt safe sharing his darker thoughts and insecurities with her. In so many ways they were kindred spirits. Both of them held back pieces of themselves from those around them.

Most people perceived him as uncomplicated and fun to hang with. He worked hard, enjoyed weekends on his boat and Charleston's nightlife. But with Sienna he'd let her glimpse what lay beneath his casual exterior. Not only had he admitted how being adopted left him feeling like an outsider, but also revealed his yearning to discover where he came from.

Would he have opened up to her if she hadn't revealed her pain at her parents' indifference? As if being a middle child wasn't hard enough, she'd been sandwiched between an older brother poised to take over the family business and a younger sister adopted because she was beautiful. Was it any wonder Sienna had retreated into intellectual pursuits that only reinforced her isolation?

What she'd disclosed about her childhood had aroused an urge to defend her against further mistreatment. Starting with the way his nameless "friend" had maligned her. For the first time since the messages began, Ethan decided to respond. He opened the most recent message he'd received from the anonymous sender and shot back a terse reply. Pouring out his frustration about all the secrecy, Ethan rebuked the sender for the vagueness of the warnings and lack of specific detail about the threat the Burns sisters represented.

Message sent, Ethan slipped on his boxer briefs and headed downstairs. He paused in the kitchen doorway to admire Sienna's sleep-mussed hair, passion-bruised lips and the appealing way her high, firm breasts filled out his shirt. Noticing his arrival, she poured a cup of coffee and came around the center island toward him. The sight of her bare legs recalled how she'd wrapped her thighs around his hips and begged him to slide deeper inside her. His erection stirred at the memory and as she neared, he wrapped his arm around her waist and eased her lower half into contact with his.

"All my favorite smells," he murmured, accepting the cup of coffee she offered, before nuzzling her neck. "Coffee, bacon and you."

He slid his lips over the spot that made her shiver. Mission accomplished, he gave her butt cheek a firm squeeze as she slid her palms over his bare chest and offered him a smoky smile.

"I thought we could use a big breakfast," she murmured, "since we missed dinner last night."

Despite having only known each other for a week, they moved in orchestrated rhythm around the kitchen, casting heated, appreciative glances at each other while they sipped coffee, poured orange juice, whipped eggs for omelets and engaged in a ritual of morning-after-great-sex kisses and casual-not-casual touches and caresses. Although they'd indulged their appetite for each other several times the previous night, his hunger for her was starting to take precedence over the emptiness of his belly. The urge to sweep the breakfast fixings off the center island so he could take her hard and fast on the granite countertop distracted him to the point where he cut his finger while slicing strawberries.

Sienna grabbed his hand and ran the cut under cold water. His chest tightened at her adorable fussing as she found a bandage to cover the minor injury. After she pronounced that he would live, he slid his fingers into her disheveled locks and dipped his head for a kiss. He'd only meant to show his appreciation for her concern, but things quickly escalated. In the end, they made good use of the space between the kitchen island and the refrigerator.

Afterward, Sienna braced her hands on Ethan's shoulders and blew out a weak chuckle. He slid his palms along her thighs and up over the curves of her butt, marveling at the peace wafting through him. This woman surprised him over and over. And it wasn't just their sexual chemistry. He noticed himself craving nothing more than to snuggle her in his arms and spend hours listening to her breathe. What was happening to him? Before a satisfactory answer came to him, Ethan's stomach growled. Sienna regarded him with a wry smile.

"Sounds like someone's worked up an appetite," she teased, easing away.

As the cooler air struck his overheated flesh, he shivered. "I can't believe we've only known each other a week," he admitted, watching her slide back into his shirt.

"I know what you mean," she admitted, gazing

at him from beneath her long lashes. A shadow of smudged mascara beneath her eyes gave her a sultry look. "I don't usually connect with people, especially men, very fast."

"So I'm special?" Ethan asked sincerely.

She looked surprised that he had to ask. "Of course you are."

"Because this feels special."

"For me, too." She expelled a shaky sigh. "To be honest I've never had such amazing sex in my life and there has to be a reason for that, right?"

"I'm new to this," Ethan admitted, hiding his conflicted feelings in vagueness.

Sienna offered him a hand up and a shy smile. "Me, too."

How was it possible that his appetite for her was so strong even as he questioned whether he could trust her? Was it the game they were engaged in that heightened his desire? He was struggling to reconcile the woman who was scheming with her sister to rob him of the future CEO position with the seemingly guileless woman who'd given herself over to their lovemaking without reservation last night and this morning. Was she that good at acting? Or was she an unwitting pawn? Either way she was dangerous. He just needed to understand if it was the risk that made her irresistible.

"What time are you meeting your mother today?" she asked, oblivious to his churning thoughts.

"She's expecting us at ten this morning."

Sienna's gaze flicked to the clock on the microwave. "Are you sure you don't want to meet with her by yourself?"

"Absolutely."

Of all the decisions that Ethan was second-guessing, following his instinct to bring Sienna along on this trip was not one of them. Despite his suspicions about what she and her sister were up to, he couldn't ignore that Sienna's presence had a steadying effect on him. And he really needed someone in his corner for this meeting.

"Are you nervous?"

"I have a lot of questions." Starting with who his father was and why his mother had believed Ethan was dead all these years.

"I imagine your mother has a lot for you, as well."

"What if I don't like her?" The words slipped out before he considered the implication. What if she didn't like him? Would they have an immediate mother/son connection or would they remain strangers torn apart by fate and unable to overcome the years of estrangement?

"I think you'll have to give yourselves a chance to get to know each other," Sienna said. "Don't expect anything and you won't be disappointed."

Ethan considered that although the advice was directed at him, it could be a reminder to herself, as well.

Nine

Sienna studied her reflection in the bathroom mirror as she put on simple pearl earrings, her mother's gift for her sixteenth birthday. She'd put a lot of thought into how she should dress for her first meeting with Ethan's mother. At first, she'd reasoned that since Carolina Gates was a businesswoman, Sienna should go with one of the expensive suits she'd brought from New York. It would broadcast that she was a career woman who could be taken seriously. On the other hand, she wasn't there to impress Carolina as much as to support Ethan, and he'd articulated his appreciation for her new style of dressing in soft fabrics that fluttered and flowed, revealing flashes of skin and highlighting her curves.

In the end she settled on a romantic dress with open

lacework details that contrasted with the demure neckline and below-the-knee skirt. When Ethan's eyes widened in admiration she twirled for him before exiting their rental, thrilled that her choice had met with his approval.

He tucked her hand into his arm in a gallant gesture as they crossed the street and entered Forsyth Park. Although the moss-draped branches of the live oaks filtered the strong morning sunlight, enough got through to make Sienna glad she was wearing a wide-brimmed hat. Tourists and residents alike flocked to the park to see the fountain or stroll the shady sidewalks that bisected the wide green expanses. Ethan and Sienna passed families with strollers, couples with cameras and numerous dog owners exercising their pets.

A ten-minute walk brought them to the wrought iron fence that surrounded the historic home where Ethan's mother lived. With her own heart pounding madly as anticipation overtook her, Sienna glanced toward Ethan to see how he was doing. His features were set in grim lines as if he was working hard to keep calm.

As they approached the gate, she could feel his tension rising. Long before their intimacy of the previous night she'd been growing ever more tuned in to his moods. She peered at his profile, noting the tightness of his mouth and the rigid set of his jaw muscles. Everything in her screamed to comfort him, to reassure him, but she hesitated to reach out.

The fear of rejection continued to plague her. Despite what had happened between them last night or how well they'd been hitting it off since she'd arrived in Charleston, they were virtual strangers. She didn't know if he'd appreciate or reject her sympathy. Yet unable to repress her concern, she bumped her shoulder against his in a spirit of comradery. The eyes he turned toward her smoldered with anxiety and excitement. Touched that he'd let her glimpse his true emotions, she gave him a reassuring smile.

"Thank you for being here." Ethan surprised her by reaching out and taking her hand in his. Squeezing her fingers gently, he added, "It means a lot to me that you were willing to come with me to do this."

"Of course." Her heart soared at his words. She'd been right to accompany him to Savannah. He was obviously more distressed than he let on. And she was honored that he would share this momentous meeting with her.

The first thing that struck Sienna as they entered the Greek Revival mansion were the modern updates to its architectural elegance. The walls, trim and original hand-carved plaster molding had been painted bright white while the honey tones of glossy heart pine flooring warmed the stark palette.

Ethan and Sienna followed the maid who answered the door into a formal parlor, with a traditional white sofa and modern chairs upholstered in navy velvet with brass frames. Between the chairs sat a bronze elephant table. Contemporary metal sculptures sat atop antique tables, and throw pillows bore an abstract watercolor design. Monochromatic curtains in a graphic pattern flanked a live-edge writing desk that sat before the window overlooking Forsyth Park.

As they settled side by side on the sofa, Sienna noticed Ethan was also studying the home as if searching for a clue to the woman who lived here. Fortunately, they didn't have long to wait before she swept into the room. Carolina Gates was a stylish woman in her early fifties who looked ten years younger. In an expensive power suit of cobalt blue, she was five feet eight inches of female empowerment. The matriarch of the Gates family wore her chocolate-brown hair brushed back from her forehead in a sleek bob that grazed her shoulders. Her keen brown eyes peered out from an unlined face.

As Carolina drew near, Ethan's grip tightened on Sienna's fingers. She answered with a squeeze of her own for reassurance. Then they were both getting to their feet and he was setting her free so he could take Carolina's outstretched hands. Mother and son stood staring at each other. Shock, grief and joy radiated from both of them. Sienna stepped to the side to give them a little space.

"You're here," Carolina announced unnecessarily, her throat working convulsively as she surveyed her son. "It's so wonderful to have you here."

"I've been looking forward to meeting you for a long time," Ethan answered, his deep voice husky, but in control.

"You're tall just like your father." Tears brightened Carolina's gaze to dazzling sharpness. "And handsome like him as well, but I think you have my nose and eyes."

Sienna's own eyes began to tear up as she observed

the poignant scene. She gave her cheek a surreptitious swipe as Carolina's gaze shifted her way.

"I'm sorry," Carolina said, nodding her greeting, obviously unwilling to let go of her son now that she'd finally gotten ahold of him. "I should've introduced myself. Carolina Gates."

"Sienna Burns."

"Her sister, Teagan, is my long-lost cousin," Ethan explained. "Finding her through the genetic testing service is what prompted me to submit my own sample."

"And I'm so glad you did," Carolina said.

"It's really nice to meet you." Sienna offered Ethan's mother a warm smile. "I hope you don't mind that I came along with Ethan."

"It's wonderful that you're here." Carolina's enchanting smile was a mirror image of her son's charming grin, while her warm brown eyes remained similarly guarded. "Sit down, both of you."

Carolina pulled Ethan toward the sofa he and Sienna had vacated, leaving Sienna to settle across from them. As if Carolina's staff had been waiting for the trio to sit down, the maid appeared with a tray containing a silver coffee service and three bone-china cups. The ritual of pouring and distributing cups of coffee gave all three a little time to assess each other and let the charged emotions ease.

"Forgive me for staring," Carolina declared with a husky laugh. "It's just that I can't believe my son is alive and sitting beside me."

"You said over the phone that you'd explain what happened."

"Straight to the point," Carolina murmured wryly. "You're definitely my son."

From the clean lines and muted tones of her decorating style, Sienna had gathered that Ethan's mother was direct and exacting. This was also reflected in her sleek hairstyle, understated makeup and the expensive sapphire-and-diamond earrings that were her only jewelry.

"Your father was the only man I ever loved. We met when I was a freshman in high school—he was two years older—and we dated for three years. When he graduated, he joined the navy and was killed in a training exercise my junior year. I didn't know until after his death that I was pregnant or we would've gotten married. My father was furious when he found out about the baby. I was an only child and he expected me to take over Gates Multimedia one day, but of course that meant attending college and getting a degree in business. How was I going to manage a rigorous class schedule at a top university while caring for an infant?"

"You said you didn't give me up, so what happened?"

"My father bribed a nurse to steal you and fake a death certificate."

An angry flush stained Ethan's cheekbones. "I was his grandchild. Why would he do that?"

"He never approved of Tony." Carolina went over to a cabinet and pulled out a scrapbook. "Antonio Bianchi," she murmured, smoothing her palm over the cover. Her features softened into an expression of such fond devotion that Sienna's heart contracted. "My father wasn't happy that I was dating someone below my social standing. Tony's family moved here from Boston. His father was a production worker for Gulf-stream Aerospace."

What would it be like to love a man so deeply that three decades of separation couldn't dim her affection? Sienna wasn't one for throwing open the doors to her heart. What had she missed because she'd played it too safe? Heartbreak obviously. But what about the highs of being in love? Observing Carolina, Sienna doubted Ethan's mother would trade in three years of loving Tony Bianchi to avoid three decades of grieving his death.

Carolina returned to her place on the sofa and opened the photo album across her knees. Pointing to one picture after another, she told the story of two young and happy lovers. Sienna's muscles relaxed as she watched Ethan, tracking his journey from wariness to bemusement and finally anguish as he realized he'd never know this man whom his mother had adored.

Slowly the overwhelming surge of emotion eased from the room and by the time lunch was announced, Ethan had recovered his equilibrium. Once again he took Sienna's hand as they went into the dining room and her heart sang at the contact even as she recognized that he sought comfort rather than romance.

"I'd love for you to come to Gates Multimedia to-morrow," Carolina began as plates of crab-stuffed ar-tichoke bottoms were placed before them. "I can give you a tour and you can meet George, Montgomery and

Byron." The husband and children of Carolina's cousin Vera who worked for the media company.

When Ethan hesitated, glancing Sienna's way before replying, she quickly piped up, "That sounds like a great idea. I really wanted to visit the Telfair Museums and worried that Ethan would be bored to tears. Sounds like this will work out best for everyone."

"Then it's settled." Carolina covered Sienna's hand with hers and gave her a grateful smile.

Warmth flooded Sienna at the older woman's friendly gesture. She found Carolina delightful and approachable. Definitely someone she'd like to spend time with and get to know better. It wasn't until Sienna's gaze shifted to Ethan that she sensed he wasn't quite as enthusiastic about his mother.

While his lips were curved into an indulgent smile, his eyes were watchful. He clearly wasn't ready to throw open the doors to his heart and invite Carolina in.

Ethan showed no inclination to linger after lunch and Sienna followed his lead, though she would've happily chatted about Carolina's collection of modern paintings for a good hour. After the older woman gave her a surprisingly demonstrative hug, Sienna allowed Ethan to lead her out the door.

After shutting the gate behind them, Ethan took her hand and whisked across the street, his long strides forcing Sienna to trot in order to keep up. Only when they'd reached the sidewalk that ran north and south through Forsyth Park did he slow his pace. Instead of heading straight back to the rental house, he detoured north past the famous fountain. As always, Sienna had scoured the internet and had dozens of facts at her disposal.

"The fountain was built in 1858 and modeled after the Place de la Concorde in Paris. Did you know it was ordered from a catalog?"

When Ethan didn't respond, Sienna glanced his way. Although their hands were linked, he was miles away. Not wanting to push him to open up to her before he was ready, she turned her attention to enjoying the play of sunlight in the water arching from the two-tiered fountain as well as the smaller sculptures around it. Yet as they resumed walking, she couldn't help but do a little deep thinking of her own about fate and the sort of difference it would've made in both Teagan's and Ethan's lives if they'd grown up surrounded by their biological families.

Sienna suspected if Teagan had grown up as a Watts, she would've found acceptance and belonging rather than criticism and judgment. Would being praised by her adoptive parents for her beauty rather than her intelligence have blunted her sister's need to win at all costs?

In Ethan's case, Sienna had learned enough about him to recognize that he used his charm as both a weapon and defense. His darker coloring isolated him in a family of blonds with blue and green eyes. No doubt he'd looked at every family photo and wondered where he truly belonged. He used his charisma and easy confidence to win every heart while never sharing his with anyone. If he'd grown up a Gates, would his grandfather's negativity have turned him pessimistic and volatile? Would he indulge in bitterness and lash out?

By the time they entered the house where they were staying, Sienna was dying to hear Ethan's thoughts on all he'd learned, but she could see that she needed to reconnect with him before that happened. Which was why she pulled him toward the stairs. She'd stripped him out of his suit coat and removed his tie before he awakened to what she was up to.

"Don't you want to go sightseeing?" He worked at the buttons of his shirt, his gaze devouring her while she slid out of her dress.

"Later," she murmured, tossing her clothes aside and stepping out of her heeled sandals. Naked, she framed his face between her palms and snared his gaze. "Right now, all I want is to make love with you."

Late Friday afternoon, Ethan returned from spending the day with his mother at Gates Multimedia. Their conversation had left him in turmoil and he was eager to share his thoughts with Sienna. Unfortunately, she hadn't returned from her tour of the historic district, so Ethan headed out to the pool with a bottle of beer and settled into a lounge chair. Usually, being around water brought clarity to his thoughts and offered him a measure of peace. Not today.

All his life he'd kept his own counsel, sharing little of his troubles with those around him, even his own family. He didn't like feeling pain so why would he want to dwell on the cause of it? But ignoring his melancholy hadn't helped. The sense of being an outsider in his own family had not diminished because he'd kept it to himself.

The last twenty-four hours had been a series of dramatic firsts. From the earthquake of making love to Sienna to meeting his birth mother and learning the truth about his past, Ethan had been hit by an unrelenting wave of charged emotions.

Sharing with Sienna his deep anguish about his grandfather's rejection had helped him process what he'd learned. His mistrust of her should've kept him from opening up fully. Especially, when he suspected she'd give Teagan ammunition against him. Yet, he couldn't stop himself from revealing the pain he'd felt over discovering that his Gates grandfather had given him away like an unwanted puppy.

"Hey." He felt Sienna's gentle touch on his shoulder, suffusing his body in warmth. "How'd it go with your mom today?"

"She offered me the CEO position with Gates Multimedia."

"Wow." Sienna perched beside him and scrutinized his expression. "That's huge."

"It totally caught me off guard."

"Not that I don't agree with her choice, but did she say why she wanted to step down?"

"She took over after her father's death with the intention of finding someone who could eventually run the company." Ethan had been surprised by Carolina's reluctance to hand over the helm to her brother-in-law or either nephew—all of whom worked for the media company.

"And now she has you."

"And now she has me." Except he wasn't convinced Gates Multimedia was where he saw himself in the future.

While Sienna headed into the kitchen to grab him another beer and fix some snacks to tide them over until dinner, Ethan grabbed his phone, intent on shooting Paul a quick message regarding Carolina's offer. When his brother had decided to start his own company instead of joining Watts Shipping, Ethan had felt obligated to step up. Now, with Teagan demonstrating an interest in the family business, Ethan was free to explore other options.

Before he began an email to Paul, Ethan scanned his inbox. Spying a familiar address, his heart began to thud.

Before you defend Sienna, you should ask her why she was blackballed from the art gallery circuit in New York.—A friend

Although Ethan was sick of the anonymous emailer's cryptic warnings, he nonetheless forwarded the message to Paul and asked his brother to check if this was true.

After that, he set aside the phone and rubbed his dry eyes as exhaustion swept over him. Why, when she seemed like the perfect lover, confidante and friend, was he constantly besieged by doubts that suggested she wasn't?

"Here you go."

At the sound of Sienna's voice, Ethan looked up to find her placing a plate loaded with crackers, cheese and fruit on the table beside him. In her other hand she held two beers.

"What are you wearing?" he asked, his gaze coasting over her bare shoulders as he accepted one of the beers.

"Don't you mean, what aren't I wearing?" With a wicked smile she whipped off the towel and dropped it on the lounge beside his.

Before Ethan gathered his scattered wits, she'd executed a flawless dive into the water. He had his shoes and shirt off before her head breached the surface.

"Aren't you coming in?" She set her feet on the pool bottom and rose out of the water like some gorgeous water nymph. His breath hitched as more and more of her pale skin appeared above the surface. A millimeter before she exposed her dusky nipples to the air, she raised her eyebrows. "The water's fine."

Ethan tossed his pants over a nearby chair, wishing it was as easy to cast aside his doubts. But when he plunged into the water and gathered Sienna's naked body into his arms, the need to protect his heart mattered less than his couldn't-stop-if-he-tried hunger to lose himself in her kisses.

Before coming to Charleston, Sienna was accustomed to choosing her wardrobe based on function rather than fun. That had changed since meeting Ethan.

She continued to marvel how his eyes lit up when she entered a room.

Awakened to the power of how the right outfit made her feel sexy and beautiful, when it came time to dress for the dinner with his family, she once again stepped outside her fashion comfort zone. She paired a full skirt of white tulle with an off-the-shoulder black lace top. Leaving her long hair flowing about her shoulders in luxurious waves, she slipped her feet into black stilettos with ankle bows and chose a black satin clutch to complete the outfit. Sienna felt confident that she'd captured a look that was partly New York and a little bit Southern.

Ethan was handsome in a lightweight gray suit and white shirt opened at the neck. As she descended the stairs, she noticed that although he appeared relaxed and smiling, his eyes remained watchful.

"I'd love for you to do me a favor tonight," he began, as he closed the front door behind them. "You can say no if it's too much to ask."

"I'm here for you. Whatever you need."

"Keep your eyes and ears open. From the way my mother spoke about everyone today, I'm wary about what I'm walking into with this family and it would really help to get your impressions of everyone."

"Of course. I'll do my best to get a sense of what they're all like."

"Thank you."

Tonight they were dining at Olde Pink House restaurant on Reynolds Square in downtown Savannah. The landmark home had been built in 1771 and went from a residence for James Habersham Jr. to a bank in 1811 and after years of neglect became a restaurant in 1992. When they arrived, Ethan and Sienna followed the hostess to the second floor where a large square table had been set before the fireplace in what had originally been the home's study. Open French doors led out to a cozy balcony where a bartender was serving cocktails.

Carolina spotted Ethan and strolled over, accompanied by a distinguished younger man who hovered possessively at her side. Carolina exuded strength and charm. She looked none the worse for the emotional encounter with her son earlier that day as she introduced her companion as Rufus Knox.

Keeping to her promise to act as Ethan's eyes and ears among his family, Sienna strolled alongside him, politely smiling as she was introduced to Carolina's cousin Vera Pruitt, her husband, George, and a trio of young women who turned out to be the girlfriend, fiancée and pregnant wife of the couple's three sons.

Met with cordial smiles that weren't exactly friendly, and from the whispering that followed in Ethan and Sienna's wake, she got the sense that Carolina's relatives weren't all that happy that they had a new family member. While Ethan fell into conversation with Carolina and Rufus, Sienna decided the best way to gather more information was to make a solo circuit of the room. Excusing herself, she headed out to the balcony to chat with Ethan's second cousins.

"Hello," she said, "I'm Sienna Burns."

The three men introduced themselves as Montgomery, Aaron and Byron. Each had their father's dirty blond hair and mother's cool hazel eyes. They were a couple inches under six feet and dressed in dapper summer-weight suits that flattered their lean, toned bodies. Surly expressions marred their classically handsome features.

"How are you enjoying Savannah?" Byron asked. His was the warmest greeting.

"Very much."

"What can you tell us about our new cousin?" Montgomery's gaze swept over her body, his interest blatant and sexual.

"What do you want to know?" Sienna asked lightly, her stomach muscles knotting in discomfort.

"Y'all are from Charleston?" Aaron drawled, swirling the bourbon in the crystal tumbler he held.

"Ethan is," she explained. "I'm from New York."

"How do you make the relationship work being so far apart from each other?" Byron asked.

"Oh, we only just met a week ago," Sienna explained. "My sister is Ethan's cousin. She just recently found out that she's related to the Wattses. She found them the same way Ethan found you all, through a genetic testing service."

Sienna went on to answer their questions about Teagan's adoption, leaving out how their mother had preferred her beautiful adopted daughter over the plain child she'd given birth to.

"Congratulations on your recent engagement," Sienna said to Montgomery, pushing her ineffectual frustration aside for the time being. "Have you set a date for your wedding?"

Aaron gave a rough laugh and clapped his brother on the shoulder. "If Hy's smart she'll tie the knot with this one before he wanders off to greener pastures."

Montgomery shot his younger brother a quelling look. "Hyacinth wants to be a June bride and needs a year to plan the wedding."

"At least," Byron muttered in amusement.

Sienna turned her gaze on Aaron. "And congratulations to you, as well. Your wife said she's due next month and that you're having a girl. Are you looking forward to being a father?"

"Is anyone?" Aaron gave another hearty laugh.

Sienna was disconcerted by his thoughtless comment and Montgomery's inappropriate regard. Was their boorish behavior a symptom of rot within their family or just a case of overcompensation because of their insecurities? She couldn't help but mark the contrast between their rudeness and the way Teagan had been welcomed with open arms by the Wattses.

"I understand your grandfather started Gates Multimedia in the late sixties," she said, to no brother in particular. "Do all of you work for the company?"

"I do," Montgomery said. "I'm the president of Gates Technology." He stated this with a pompous air, then tipped his glass to indicate the youngest brother. "Byron is the regional manager for our broadcast network on the West Coast and our father is CFO."

"Carolina is lucky to have so many family members that she can count on." No one seemed to hear the irony in her voice so she turned to Aaron and asked, "What is it you do?"

Montgomery spoke up before his brother could. "Aaron has dabbled in quite a few ventures, but hasn't found anything that suits him."

Deep resentment filled the gaze Aaron directed at his brother. "I'm between projects at the moment."

After making both his brothers uncomfortable, a satisfied smile twisted Montgomery's lips. "And what is it you do?"

Sienna explained her business, and then went a step further and shared her sister's early business successes, all the while wondering if she imagined the surprise on both their faces. There was no question in her mind that their mother and romantic partners were not interested in pursuing careers. They came from wealthy families and while they might have dabbled in some sort of work, once they settled on a husband, they intended on dedicating all their energies to being the perfect wife and mother.

Did it bother them that the person in charge at Gates Multimedia was a woman?

At dinner, Sienna found herself seated between Byron and Montgomery. As everyone sat down, Sienna noticed that while she and Ethan had been expertly separated, the rest of the assembled couples had remained paired up. Divide and conquer? She caught Ethan's eye and noted that he too had recognized the ploy. A thrill went through her at their silent communication. It seemed implausible that they'd only met a week ago and yet their minds were already operating along similar lines. Or maybe it was just wishful thinking on her part.

The last person with whom she'd developed a quick and powerful connection had been her best friend, Gia. The two had immediately clicked freshman year and supported each other through four years of college and beyond. Sienna couldn't imagine her life without Gia in it. If that was the same attachment she was developing with Ethan, what changes did her future hold? What if their relationship was a one-sided affair? She'd heard enough stories of Ethan's romantic escapades to recognize that he wasn't the sort to commit. Was she on the verge of putting too much of herself into their affair only to end up disappointed and hurt?

Montgomery raised his eyebrows. "So you and our cousin aren't dating?"

Caught off guard by the blunt question, Sienna's cheeks heated beneath Montgomery's scrutiny. What label did she apply to their romance when she wasn't sure where things were headed? "We're...friends."

"Seems like there's a little bit more to it." Montgomery's gaze dropped to her lips and then lowered to her breasts. "Or maybe he doesn't know a good thing when it's right under his nose."

Sienna's cheeks heated even as outrage surged through her. Surely the man couldn't be hitting on her with his fiancée sitting beside him. She glanced to where Hyacinth was deep in conversation with her future father-in-law before glancing across the table and noticing Ethan's stony gaze fixed on Montgomery. Had he seen the interaction and wondered what was going on? His displeasure worried her. The last thing she wanted to do was cause trouble between Ethan and his new relatives.

"We understand Ethan and his father work for Watts Shipping," Byron began as soon as the waiter had taken their drink orders.

Sienna saw past the younger man's polite curiosity to the concern that Carolina's newfound son might be interested in joining Gates Multimedia and the detrimental consequences that could have on their futures.

"At the moment," she said. "His grandfather was chairman of the board until his stroke a few months back. He's been steadily improving and has taken back some of his duties."

"But he has a brother and several cousins," Byron continued. "They don't have any interest in the family business?"

As long as she stuck to public information, Sienna saw no harm in answering these questions. "His brother, Paul, owns a cybersecurity company. Ethan also has twin cousins. One is a chef, the other a hairdresser."

"It sounds as if Ethan is the one most likely to run his family's company in the future," Montgomery piped up, exchanging a satisfied glance with his brother.

"I wouldn't know." Sienna thought about the panic that would set in with her dinner companions if she mentioned Teagan's ambition regarding Watts Shipping. "But it seems as if that would make sense."

The waiter brought their drinks, and Sienna took the opportunity to change the subject. The rest of the dinner was an ordeal as she parried questions about Ethan, declaring that they'd only known each other a short time and his cousins would be better off asking him directly. She continuously redirected the conversation to generic topics like the city of Savannah and got them to discuss their own lives.

She discovered Byron and his girlfriend, Melinda, had gone to the same high school, but hadn't begun dating until after college. The pretty redhead was the most down-to-earth of all the women involved with the Pruitt boys. Montgomery deferred to his fiancée about their upcoming wedding and Hyacinth's plans carried them through the dessert course.

When no one seemed eager to linger over coffee, Sienna was thrilled to bid her dinner companions goodbye, assure Carolina how nice it had been to meet her and escape to the powder room. By the time she reached the sidewalk outside the restaurant, Ethan was standing alone and frowning at his cell phone. He was so absorbed that he didn't notice her approach until she spoke.

"Is something wrong?"

His head whipped up and he shoved the phone into his pocket. "Not a thing."

"Are you sure? You look upset."

At first the smile he offered her seemed a little strained around the edges, but after he wrapped his arm around her waist and deposited a sizzling kiss on her lips, she lost track of her concern.

"Let's get out of here," he murmured against her

ear. "It's our last night in Savannah and I want it to be memorable."

Sienna tunneled her fingers into his thick hair and let her kiss communicate her total agreement to that plan.

Ten

Sunday morning, Ethan left Sienna slumbering and crossed Forsyth Park to have breakfast with his mother. He was no more eager to have a conversation about her offer to join Gates Multimedia than he was to deal with the ongoing battle between his ever-increasing emotional attachment to Sienna and the events—pointed to by the anonymous caller and confirmed last night by Paul—that depicted her as a liar and a cheat. If she'd been any other woman, Ethan would've immediately ended their association. But the thought of never seeing Sienna again aroused an ache that couldn't be wished or willed away.

Entering his mother's house, Ethan pushed Sienna to the back of his mind and followed the maid into the dining room where Carolina sat in a voluminous caftan, sipping coffee. He greeted her and sat down, smiling absently as she poured him a cup from the coffeepot beside her and handed it over.

"Thank you for last night's dinner," she began, a warm expression in her brown eyes. "I think everyone enjoyed themselves."

"I'm glad to hear that." On the way over Ethan had debated whether to continue the fiction that all was well, or to come clean about his thoughts. "Although I suspect not everyone was happy to welcome a new family member." If he hadn't kept a close eye on his mother's reaction, he might've missed her microgrimace. "They already suspect you've invited me to join the company."

"You're my son. The company should be yours."

Ethan resisted a grimace of his own. He didn't want to shut any doors, but what she was offering him could change everything. And not necessarily for the better. "I appreciate where you're coming from, but you barely know me. And there's my position at Watts Shipping to consider. I can't just walk away and leave them hanging."

Yet wasn't that exactly what he could do? With Teagan actively working to take away what all along had been his, it would be the perfect solution for everyone. Nor could he ignore how long he'd been pondering an opportunity like what his mother was offering. So what accounted for his resistance?

"I understand that this is all very sudden," Carolina said. "All I'm asking is for you to give it some thought.

Maybe come down and spend some time with me getting to know the business. See if you like it."

Her request was completely reasonable and despite the disquiet roiling in his gut, Ethan found himself agreeing to do just that. The conversation shifted to a discussion of his cousins. Carolina had a lot to say about Montgomery's upcoming wedding and Aaron's pending fatherhood. Despite her attempts to sound positive, Ethan could tell she wasn't fully sold on any of the Pruitt siblings, although she seemed most optimistic about Byron.

They lingered over breakfast longer than Ethan intended and he suddenly realized the time to head back to Charleston was fast approaching. His mother escorted him to the front door and bid him goodbye with a sad smile. Her forlorn expression made him regret that he couldn't stay a few more days. Before heading out, Ethan impulsively bent to kiss her cheek, the first show of affection he'd initiated. Eyes bright with unshed tears, Carolina set her fingertips over the spot and watched from the doorway as he headed down the walk.

Light-headed, with heart thumping madly in his chest, he crossed the street. His emotional response to leaving Carolina plagued him as he strode across the park. The gush of fondness felt like a betrayal of the woman who'd raised him. He barely knew Carolina and it was certainly too soon for him to claim he loved her, but some emotion had him solidly in its grip.

After entering the house, Ethan completed a quick circuit of both floors and found no sign of Sienna. No doubt she was taking one final stroll around the historic district. He shook off the niggling disappointment at her absence. When had he become a man who craved the company of one particular woman? The answer followed him into the bedroom they'd shared.

Sienna's voice reached his ears as he collected his charger from the nightstand. She was in the courtyard behind the house. Opening the door that led to the back terrace, Ethan was about to let her know he was back when he realized who was on the other end of the call.

"Honestly, Teagan," Sienna said, "this is a huge deal and you absolutely can't tell anyone in the family about it."

Even though he wasn't surprised Sienna had betrayed him to her sister, he was astonished how much it hurt. Counting on her to have his back had been a risk, especially with what he'd been warned to expect from Teagan.

"Because no one knows." Sienna's reply was everything Ethan had been dreading. "He hasn't said anything to his family yet."

In a weak attempt to change the topic, Sienna started going on about all that she'd seen around town.

"Savannah's a bit different from Charleston. The historic district contains more than twenty squares and several churches. The house we're staying at is across from Forsyth Park and I've visited a couple really nice museums."

Obviously, Teagan wasn't to be distracted because after a momentary pause to listen, Sienna dropped all talk of Savannah.

"I think it's a little premature to talk about whether or not Ethan's going to inherit," Sienna responded in a quelling tone.

Silence filled the courtyard for several seconds before Sienna spoke again.

"If Ethan became CEO of Gates Multimedia, that would make things a lot easier for you, wouldn't it? Then the way would be clear for you to be the CEO of Watts Shipping."

Ethan hadn't really needed the warning emails. Teagan hadn't exactly been subtle about learning all about Watts Shipping's operations, and then demonstrating her business savvy in lengthy conversations with the current CEO. His dad had taken several of her suggestions under advisement and Grady, current chairman of the board, was singing her praises.

Still, it wasn't Teagan's machinations that bothered him at the moment, but the information she was receiving from Sienna. Caught up in meeting his birth family, he'd forgotten to be wary.

"Sure," Sienna said bitterly. "It's a win-win for everybody."

In the silence following her statement, Ethan's thoughts whirled. While Teagan's eagerness to poach his position at Watts Shipping annoyed him to no end, he couldn't deny the simplicity of her suggestion.

"And if he doesn't want to work for Gates Multimedia?" Sienna asked, letting her annoyance come through loud and clear. "I should convince him?"

Lost in the passion of their strong sexual connection, he'd lost track of her role in her sister's schemes.

"You're crazy if you believe that he's into me that much."

Ethan pondered Teagan's opinion and considered how he'd been feeling these last few days. His gut clenched when he remembered Sienna's hands roaming hungrily over him. Her passionate kisses. The sexy sounds she made. The thought of all that incredible sex being a vehicle for Teagan's ambition made him sick.

"He's not falling in love with me," Sienna protested, sounding oddly withdrawn. "I don't care what his family says."

Ethan's hands balled into fists. That his family had been speculating about his feelings for Sienna didn't surprise him. Nor was he shocked that Teagan had encouraged her sister to capitalize on how smitten he appeared to be about her.

But Sienna confiding his private business to her sister after he requested she not reveal the information until he could share it with his parents was a betrayal he couldn't stomach. Especially not when he was poised on the brink of falling for her.

Ethan had heard enough. He eased the French door closed and retreated. In so many ways, it was almost a relief to have his suspicions confirmed. Now he could stop worrying about fighting whatever emotions had begun to develop. Proof of her deception meant that he wouldn't give her a second thought when she returned to New York. Even before she'd shown her true colors, the possibility that anything between them could survive beyond these couple weeks had been crazy. Their interlude had been a means to an end. A way to keep tabs on what Teagan was up to.

Today's overheard conversation demonstrated why he'd developed a relationship with Sienna. Now that he was in possession of valuable insight about how Teagan intended to use her sister, he was free to do whatever it took to mislead his rival.

The weekend in Savannah was fast becoming a precious memory as the city vanished in the distance behind them. Sienna sat in the passenger seat beside Ethan and fought back melancholy. The intense connection that had developed during their time together these past few days had surpassed anything she'd ever experienced. Being with him as he'd navigated the emotional storm of meeting his birth mother and his blood relatives had connected them at a spiritual level she hadn't expected. The glimpse of his fears and insecurities had allowed Sienna to drop her guard. With their true selves exposed, they'd come together in bed with feverish urgency and the sex had blown her mind.

And now they were heading back to Charleston and she had to face the fact it was almost over. Already, she'd lingered beyond the original few days she'd planned to stay. All too soon she would be heading back to New York City. Back to isolation and the grind of long days spent flying around the world, brutally awakened to the realization that filling her hours with work wasn't the solution to loneliness.

She glanced at Ethan's profile. Maybe that could change. He hadn't come out and declared that he wanted to see more of her, and she might be kidding herself that he had felt anything for her beyond desire, but the fact that he'd invited her to Savannah said something. But now, with Ethan being so uncharacteristically silent, Sienna wondered if she was on his mind at all.

Before they'd left, he'd gone alone to have breakfast with his mother and said little since returning. No doubt leaving Carolina was difficult after having just found her. Or had he made a decision about her offer to join Gates Multimedia? He'd shut her down when she'd asked, claiming he had a lot of thinking to do.

Despite her spinning thoughts, Sienna must've dozed because the next thing she knew the car wasn't moving. Blinking to clear the fog from her brain, she lifted her head off the passenger window and spied the curved double steps leading to the front door of Grady's estate.

Covering a yawn, she turned her head toward Ethan. "Sorry." The word died on her lips as she noticed his expression. "What's wrong?"

"What's wrong?" he snarled, gaze slashing her way. He gripped the steering wheel with one hand and pointed his phone at her with the other. "Your sister. That's what."

Sienna's heart sank. Had Teagan succeeded in accomplishing her goal? Was she going to be the next CEO of Watts Shipping?

"What did she do?" Sienna whispered.

"As if you don't know."

"It's Teagan," she muttered. "There are any number of things she could get up to."

"She told my parents that I went to Savannah to meet with Carolina."

"Oh, no."

"Don't act so shocked," he said in disgust. "You knew she knew."

"I—"

Breath hissing through her teeth in dismay, Sienna closed her eyes and tried to think. What could she say to defuse the situation without lying to him? She'd suspected that Teagan wouldn't keep the information to herself. Why hadn't she warned Ethan that her sister knew all about Carolina and Gates Multimedia? Because she loved her sister and was falling for Ethan. Trying to keep both of them happy when they were competing for the same job was doomed to fail.

"I heard you on the phone with her," Ethan continued. "You were telling her all about my birth mother and Gates Multimedia."

"I didn't tell her anything." Her lungs worked as if she was running full out. She couldn't seem to gather enough breath to make her case. "She already knew."

"You expect me to believe that?" His sarcastic tone lashed at her. "Only you and Paul knew and he didn't blab to her."

The fact that Teagan had known the real reason for their trip to Savannah demonstrated her sister had found others besides Sienna to do her bidding. Who besides her and Paul could've spilled the beans?

"I swear she knew." This was her chance to set

him straight, to declare herself a victim of Teagan's actions, to fight for...what? Every kiss. Every touch. Every murmured endearment between them. It had all been amazing, but what was between them was destined to end even before this conversation. "I'd never do that to you."

I care about...you.

More than any other man she'd ever known. The reality of it struck her hard.

"And I'm just supposed to believe you?" He scoffed.

"It's true."

"You don't seriously think I'm going to take your word for it." His icy manner was a shock to her system. "Especially not after your sister asked you to convince me to leave Watts Shipping and go to work for Gates Multimedia."

Sienna appreciated that he had every right to be irritated with Teagan's scheming. And by keeping quiet about her sister's plans, Sienna had in effect sided with Teagan. The secret had become harder and harder to maintain as her feelings for Ethan had developed. How long before she would've confessed the truth? And at what cost to both her relationship with Teagan and her budding romance with Ethan?

"Would that be so terrible?" Sienna hated that he was right to doubt her. "It's a fantastic opportunity."

"And it benefits your sister."

"It benefits you both. You told me how you'd been feeling like an outsider lately. That you weren't sure how or if you fit with the Wattses anymore. I thought that meeting Carolina and seeing how happy she was to have you in her life was exactly what you'd been missing. Her suggestion that you take over the company is just icing on the cake."

For a long time he stared at her in silence. "I turned down my mother's offer to run Gates Multimedia."

His declaration set off a bomb of anxiety inside her. "Being welcomed by your family. Becoming CEO of Gates Multimedia. Isn't this exactly what you hoped for? Or am I wrong?"

"That's what I let you think."

With the revelation that he'd overheard her talking to Teagan, a dramatic shift had occurred in the way he was behaving toward her. Or had it? *That's what I let you think.* Had he been lying to her all this time? Disarming her with his irresistible smiles and seducing her to keep her off-balance? Sienna flushed with humiliation. Had she really been duped so easily? Had he been laughing at her this whole time? Flattering the unattractive sister until she believed he could truly want her?

"What you let me think?" she echoed, wishing that she'd heard him wrong. "Why?"

"I knew what Teagan was up to from the start."

Sienna's stomach dropped to her toes.

She decided to play dumb for the moment. "What Teagan is up to?"

"Your sister wants to run Watts Shipping."

Since lying would only get her into more trouble, Sienna gave a reluctant nod. "Teagan is one of the most ambitious people I know. And once she gets something into her head—"

"Never mind that I have ten years of experience and she knows nothing about shipping."

Sienna made a helpless gesture. "Her determination to take over Watts Shipping has nothing to do with your qualifications."

"Then what is it exactly?" Ethan demanded.

"You have to understand where she's coming from. She thinks that she deserves to run the company because…" Sienna gulped, horrified at having to explain her sister's reasoning. "Because she's related by blood and you're—"

"Adopted." Beneath Ethan's bleak tone lurked more pain than he'd ever let her see before and Sienna's stomach wrenched.

Overcome by regret at the misery she was causing him, Sienna sank her nails into her palms and soldiered on. "She has her reasons for thinking that way."

"I'm sure."

Sienna found herself in the exact position she'd been dreading, caught between her familial loyalty to Teagan and her new and shockingly fierce feelings for Ethan. Now, faced with his anger and criticism, she stumbled and fell into the familiar habit of making excuses for Teagan.

"Our father refused to let her run the family company and she believes it's because she's adopted." Sienna rushed through the explanation, hoping that Ethan's own experiences would allow him to understand what Teagan was going through. Of all the things she had shared with Ethan, she'd avoided discussing her sister's insecurities with him. "That's not the reason though. Aiden might not be the best choice to take over, but he's firstborn and a son. My father is quite traditional that way. He wouldn't have let me run the company if I wanted to either."

Ethan looked utterly unmoved by her explanation. "You always stick up for her, don't you?"

"She's my sister."

"Yes," he mused, his disapproval plain. "So what's your plan now that you know that I'm not going to leave Watts Shipping?"

"I don't think Teagan will succeed in taking Watts Shipping away from you."

"Are you willing to help make sure that's the case?"

Sienna shifted her gaze and stared miserably out the windshield. For the last three days she'd been the happiest woman alive. While it seemed unfair that her relationship with Ethan had to implode like this, she should've expected that standing with one foot on the boat and the other on the dock would be treacherous.

"Please don't ask me to get in the middle of this."

"But you're already there. Whose side are you on, Sienna? Will you keep quiet that I know what she's up to? Or are you going to continue doing her bidding?"

"Her bidding?" Sienna echoed, bile rising in her throat. Suddenly, she was thrown back to high school and all the times her sister had used her in some meticulously plotted scheme. Those days, she hadn't been strong enough to resist or outthink her sister. "What exactly is it you think I've done?"

"It's pretty obvious."

"Not to me." She scanned his expression while her

thoughts raced frantically. "I'll admit that I knew that she was determined to be the next CEO, but I never said or did anything to you or any of your family to help her."

Ethan looked completely unmoved. "Of course you'd deny it—"

"It's the truth," Sienna interrupted, frustration boiling up in her. Seeing his doubt, she continued, "Okay, fine. Maybe I had very selfish motives for encouraging you to accept your mother's offer. I'd hoped if you became the CEO of Gates Multimedia and Teagan ran Watts Shipping then both of you could be happy." And her heart wouldn't be torn in two. "But now I'm starting to see that neither of you gives a damn about being happy. You both just want to win."

"*We* want to win?" Ethan snorted derisively. "That's hilarious coming from someone who has done the things you have."

"What things?"

"I know that you've overinflated the value of a painting to increase your commission and that you've hired someone to bid on something at auction to drive up the price your client will receive."

Sienna recoiled from the accusation, her insides turning to ice. Was someone deliberately feeding him lies or had he twisted events from her past to substantiate that he was right to mistrust her? Fumbling with the handle, Sienna managed to open the door, but before she could exit the car, Ethan's long fingers wrapped around her wrist. His grip was firm, a hair's breadth from painful.

"If you believe all these terrible things about me," she panted, desperate to escape him before the tears blurring her vision turned into full-on sobbing, "then why didn't you confront me about this sooner?"

"Because I didn't want you to know I was onto you and your sister."

She thought about the long hours she'd spent in his arms. The sex had been fierce and hungry. With their time together shrinking, she believed he'd been equally distressed that they'd soon be parting. Instead, the whole time they'd been intimate, he'd viewed her with such contempt.

Before despair immobilized her, she pushed away such thoughts. "You found out how?"

"That's not important."

"It is important because if you had Paul investigate me then you'd know that's not who I am."

Ethan's expression hardened to granite. "It was someone anonymous."

"So, some unnamed source spews vile lies about me and you just believe it?" Her voice grew screechy as her throat closed up. "After everything... I just... I can't..."

What the hell was happening? Frantic to escape, she yanked against his grip. Her despair was reaching a fever pitch when he set her free so suddenly that she practically tumbled out of the car. Without a backward glance, she raced up the entry stairs, not caring that she'd left her laptop and her suitcase behind.

Eleven

Ethan entered the two-story, L-shaped house where he and Paul had grown up. Passing beneath the elegant arch that led into the formal parlor, he stepped straight into hell.

Usually walking into the home was like being enveloped in a comforting hug. Not today. His parents' penetrating stares sent a bone-deep chill through him before he'd taken more than three steps into the room.

They must've known he was on his way because his mother sat in a straight-back chair rather than her favorite spot on the sofa, her spine ramrod straight. His father stood just behind her, his hand resting on her shoulder. Their position was a clear warning that they'd allied against him.

"I'm sorry," Ethan began, rushing forward with an apology even as his feet stopped moving.

"We're very disappointed that you didn't think you could come to us," Miles Watts intoned, the deep throb in his voice broadcasting his sadness.

"I was going to tell you." Ethan clenched his teeth against the frustration rising in him. The absolute last thing he wanted was to be in his current mess.

"When exactly?" his father asked.

"As soon as I got back from Savannah."

"Did you give any thought to how difficult it was going to be for your mother and me to hear about this from someone other than you?"

"Of course. This is the last thing I wanted." That it had been Teagan who'd spilled the beans thanks to the information provided by Sienna made it all the worse. "Teagan had no business saying anything."

"She didn't appear to realize we hadn't been told."

Ethan gathered breath to dispute that. He knew perfectly well that only this morning Sienna had asked her sister not to say anything. That an hour later Teagan had spilled the beans over brunch to his entire family was one more reason she would never be in charge of Watts Shipping. They didn't need someone with such poor character at the helm.

"I wasn't the one who told Teagan," Ethan said. "It was Sienna."

"Why are you surprised? You brought her sister with you to Savannah," Miles pointed out. "Surely the two of them discussed why."

"I asked her not to say anything to anyone."

"So you trusted her with your news," his mother said, speaking up for the first time. *But you didn't trust us.* The implication sliced into Ethan.

What could he say? His reasons for confiding in Sienna seemed the height of stupidity now that she'd betrayed him. Leaning on her support hadn't felt risky while they were in Savannah. Their closeness during the trip had even led to him defending her to the anonymous emailer. What an idiotic thing to do.

"We've spent a lot of time together this last week."

Something about this seemed to take his mother aback. "I see."

"None of this changes the fact that you told a virtual stranger before you shared it with us," his father added.

His father labeling Sienna a stranger bothered Ethan more than it should. Granted, strong sexual chemistry didn't necessarily translate into a relationship, but there'd been moments when he felt they'd made a true connection.

Too bad it had been one great big lie.

"Searching for your birth mother was a huge decision," his mother said. "I don't understand why you didn't feel like you could come to us."

"I know I should've said something..."

"Did you think we wouldn't approve?" his father demanded, eyebrows lowering.

"No." Ethan rubbed the back of his neck. "Of course not."

Lies. Even now, confronted by his parents' despair, he couldn't be honest. What was he afraid of? That they'd reject him? Tell him that he was no longer part

of their family? The pain that blasted through him indicated that's exactly what he feared.

How was that even possible? They'd done nothing
except make him feel loved and included. The problem was his. The insecurity fabricated by his mind.

"Then what?" Miles thundered.

Constance gripped her husband's hand as if to rein
him in. "What your father is trying to say is that we're
struggling with this big secret you kept from us."

"I didn't want to upset you for no reason if nothing
came of the testing."

Miles sighed. "It would've been nice to know what
you were going through."

"Maybe we could've helped." Constance was trying to look brave, but her lips quivered with suppressed
emotion. "Why don't you start at the beginning and
explain the best you can," his mother said, loving concern resonating in her voice. "When did you decide to
look for your birth mom?"

"It happened when Lia was pretending to be Ava's
daughter," Ethan began. "When Grady decided to try
the genetic testing service, I started thinking about sub-
mitting my DNA, as well. I don't know that I actually
expected to be matched with anyone."

Miles grunted. "If that was the case then I'd like to
think you could've come to us."

"I wanted to." Ethan grimaced. Why hadn't he taken
Paul's advice and told them right away? "I should've."

"But you didn't," his father pointed out. "And I'm
sure you can see how much that worries us."

The stark disappointment in his father's eyes made

Ethan feel like a child who'd misbehaved. His parents had never yelled or punished. They'd always explained what he'd done wrong and calmly discussed the consequences for his actions.

"I never set out to hurt you."

"We know that," his mother said, blinking rapidly.

"I just needed some time to meet my birth mother and sort out how I was feeling." Ethan badly wanted to go to his mother and feel her fingers stroke his hair like when he was little and Paul had gone out to play with his friends, leaving Ethan behind. The memory startled him. Ethan hadn't thought about how it felt to be abandoned by his brother in a long time.

"How were you feeling?" his mother asked, her voice so low he almost missed it. "What was going on that you couldn't come to us?"

Ethan swallowed. He'd been trying to avoid telling his parents the truth. Would they understand that his feelings of being an outsider had nothing to do with them or how they'd raised him?

"I was restless. Out of sorts." How could he make them understand? Especially when he wasn't so sure what was going on himself. "I kept thinking that I didn't fit in. I don't look like any of you."

"Why does that matter?" his father asked.

"You are one of us though. A Watts through and through," his mother put in. "You know that, right?"

When Ethan remained silent, grappling with how to clarify things, his mother spoke up again.

"You can't possibly think that because you are adopted, you aren't part of this family."

"Everything is about legacy in Charleston. Who your blood family is matters more than what you've done or how rich you are. It isn't a place that welcomes outsiders. No one can buy their way in. Being adopted makes me feel like I don't truly belong. I didn't mean for you to think you aren't the two most amazing parents a guy could have."

He added this last as his mother had gone quite pale.

"We understand." Miles took his wife's hands and offered her support. "But realize when you choose not to trust us with what you're going through that it seems as if we've failed you in some way."

"You haven't failed me." This was the exact scenario Ethan had hoped to avoid. He'd known his parents wouldn't understand his motivation when he was having such a difficult time wrapping his own head around it. "If anyone has messed up it's me."

"Don't say that."

The agony in his mother's eyes shredded Ethan's heart. Helpless to stop his mother's misery, Ethan focused all his frustration on the woman who'd caused this problem. This was all Sienna's fault. If she had just kept her mouth shut, he could've been the one to tell his parents. Instead they'd been blindsided.

"You know my birth mom will never be more important to me then you and Dad."

Only he could see neither one believed him. No matter how vigorous his assurances, the words came too late. The damage was done. His parents felt betrayed and there was no undoing it. Ethan could only hope that with time they might forgive him.

"Of course we know that," Miles said, his words belying the lines of stress bracketing his mouth and the death grip on his wife's hand. "And we hope you know that if we're upset it's only because we're worried about you."

"What is she like?" his mother asked.

"Carolina?" Ethan swallowed hard. How did he explain the feeling of homecoming when he met her? Or the closure he received finding out why she hadn't raised him? "She runs Gates Multimedia. Never married and never had any more children. The man she loved—my father—died in a training accident. He was in the navy."

Although Ethan knew he was coming at his mother's question sideways, he hadn't yet taken the time to process his feelings.

"Oh, Ethan." His mother looked stricken. "I'm so sorry to hear that your father died."

"What prompted your...birth mother to try to find you after all this time?" Miles asked.

Ethan explained the circumstances surrounding his birth and what his grandfather had done. His mother clapped her hand over her mouth and regarded him with horrified eyes.

"We had no idea," his father said. "It was a closed adoption and we trusted the lawyer that everything was done in a legal manner."

With this reassurance, something unraveled inside Ethan. He didn't realize until now that since discovering the circumstances surrounding his adoption, he'd been afraid his parents had been in on the scheme.

Some of this must've shown in his face because his father scowled.

His mother got to her feet and came over to wrap her arms around him. "We're happy you found your birth mother," she whispered, her voice urgent. "She is lucky to have you back in her life."

Ethan hugged her tight and realized for the first time in a long time that he felt at peace. How ironic to discover that he had to figure out where he'd come from in order to know who he was and where he wanted to be.

Heartbroken following her fight with Ethan and angry with herself for giving up when she should've fought harder to defend herself and get to the bottom of the anonymous accusations, Sienna sobbed herself to exhaustion, fell asleep and woke after dark with a headache and an empty stomach. Feeling like an intruder, she snuck down to the kitchen, quickly made herself a sandwich and then fled back to the guest room. To her relief, she met no one coming or going. Still, she wondered how long she could stay before someone decided she was the root of all evil and kicked her out.

Before that happened, she would pack and make arrangements to fly back to New York. First thing tomorrow, if at all possible. It was imperative that she get the hell out of Charleston. Not just for her sanity, but because once again she'd done what she'd sworn she wouldn't. She'd neglected her business and given Teagan her full support. Which once again resulted in her getting kicked in the head and feeling as if her whole body was one big raw nerve.

It wasn't until she got back to her room and threw open the armoire that she remembered the last time she'd seen her luggage: it was in the trunk of Ethan's car. With a heavy sigh, she headed back downstairs. To her relief, she found her suitcase and laptop just inside the front door. Grabbing everything, she headed back upstairs. As she reached the second floor, bumping her heavy suitcase up the steps made enough noise to draw Teagan from her room.

"Are you just getting back?" her sister asked, eyeing the luggage.

"No. I just hadn't brought my bag upstairs." Sienna didn't pause as she spoke, but headed for the next flight of steps.

"So…" Teagan trailed after her. "Is Ethan going to take the position with his mother's company?"

It was on the tip of Sienna's tongue to tell Teagan what Ethan had shared with her, but wasn't that exactly the sort of thing he'd accused her of doing? Helping Teagan in her bid to become the next CEO of Watts Shipping? Well, she would eventually find out what Ethan had decided.

"I think you should ask him that question."

"He didn't tell you?"

Sienna's irritation spiked, but she waited until they reached her room before venting her frustration. Swinging her suitcase onto the bed, she whirled to face her sister. "Why did you tell Ethan's family about meeting his birth mother after I specifically told you not to?"

"They deserved to know."

"That wasn't your call."

Teagan waved her hand as if Sienna's irritation was a cloud of smoke that offended her. "Why are you acting all huffy? You knew from the beginning that I intended to beat him out for the CEO position. Whatever it took."

"He accused me of telling you." Sienna narrowed her gaze. "You never did explain how you found out."

"It's not important."

"It is to me." Sienna found herself on the verge of tears and ground her teeth in frustration. "He thinks I betrayed him."

"I can't reveal my source," Teagan said. "If I do, they won't be useful to me anymore."

"Like I've been useful? This whole time you didn't give a damn what it meant to me that Ethan and I were hitting it off. You deliberately let me think he was interested so you could get the inside track to Ethan." Sienna paused to glare at her sister, hoping that Teagan would deny it. When her sister gave an offhanded shrug, Sienna growled. "You are the worst."

Driven by a burning need to get as far away from Charleston and her sister as possible, Sienna crossed to the armoire and began unloading its contents onto the bed.

"Did you seriously think I would ignore the opportunity presented when Ethan found you attractive?"

"I guess not." She'd known better than to trust her sister's motives, yet she'd allowed herself to be sucked in. Despair filled her. "But for once I guess I hoped you'd be happy for me because a man I was attracted to liked me in return."

"And you had fun, didn't you?" Teagan shoved Sienna's suitcase aside, disrupting her neat piles of clothes in the process, and plopped onto the bed. "I mean, come on, the guy is gorgeous and charming and I'll bet he's great in—"

"I really care about him," Sienna interrupted, shocking herself at the admission.

Teagan's eyes went wide. "You've known him a little over a week."

Had she really believed her sister would give a damn? Why did it have to be stupid and foolish to wish Teagan would support her for a change?

Opening the second suitcase, she began to fill it, packing as if her life depended on being done in the next ten minutes.

"What are you doing?" Teagan demanded, her gaze flying from the armoire to the suitcases and finally to Sienna.

"Packing."

"I can see that. But why?"

"I have work waiting for me in New York."

"You can't leave. I need you here."

That summed up Sienna's reality. When it came to her sister, their relationship was a one-way street with all lanes flowing toward Teagan.

"Did you miss the part where Ethan blames me for what you did?" To her dismay, Sienna found herself choking up and forced down her misery. She would absolutely, positively not cry after becoming her sister's victim once more. She would return to Manhattan and throw herself back into her career, putting Charleston and Ethan Watts in her rearview mirror. "It's over between us and I'm devastated. For the first time in your life, why don't you try thinking about someone beside yourself?"

"I am. These people have been looking for me for decades."

"These people? They're your family." Sienna stopped throwing clothes willy-nilly into her suitcase and stared at her sister. "Why did you come here? You obviously don't give a damn about any of them."

"It's not that I don't care about them." To Teagan's credit, she looked visibly upset. "I don't know them."

Sienna's heart melted. "So get to know them. After all, you've been searching for them for years. Appreciate that you have relatives who love you. Aunts and uncles and cousins who don't want anything from you. They're just happy to have you in their lives. Can't you feel the same way?"

"Ugh. You just don't get it." Teagan spoke brusquely as if she hadn't listened to anything Sienna had just said. "If you don't want to help me then just go back to New York. I'll figure out something else."

Sienna didn't realize how much she hoped her words would get through to her sister until that bubble burst. An ache started in her heart and spread throughout her body. Was it possible that Teagan's obsession with controlling and dominating everything in her life had rendered her blind to the risk of losing everyone who loved her?

"Come with me," Sienna tried again. Reaching for her sister's hand, she squeezed her fingers in a fierce grip.

"You just don't get it," Teagan complained, wrenching away from her. "I don't belong in New York anymore."

Following her sister's drama-filled exit, Sienna puzzled over Teagan's impassioned declaration. What had Teagan meant? She was way more suited to New York City than Charleston. Between her social life and her wildly successful businesses, the Big Apple was Teagan's oyster. In contrast, Charleston's pace and old-school style were at odds with Teagan's trendsetting ways.

Was this about her being passed over for Burns Properties? The lengths to which Teagan was going to become the next CEO of Watts Shipping seemed to point to her needing a confidence boost. That being said, manipulating situations to her advantage was the exact sort of thing that her sister thrived on. Even before she could speak, Teagan had deployed her big green eyes and sweet smile to win the hearts of everyone she met. And if charm didn't work, she wielded her clever mind like an assassin, taking out her opponents by clandestine means.

Sienna knew better than to trust her sister and had spent her entire life avoiding her sister's machinations. Why had she picked now to turn a blind eye to the potential fallout of her sister's scheming?

Because she'd fallen in love.

Logic went out the window when the heart was involved. As things had heated up between them, she'd fallen prey to the fantasy of a future with a man who turned her on and made her happy. Naturally, she believed Teagan's assurances that Ethan was developing feelings for her. Sienna had been desperate for that to be true.

With her new suitcases crammed to the point of bursting, Sienna booked herself on the earliest flight back to New York the following day and got ready for bed.

Twelve

"I hear congratulations are in order," Teagan said, strolling into Ethan's office.

Ethan flipped a glance toward his cousin. With her signature confidence, she strode toward his desk as if she had already been named CEO. Today Teagan wore her version of a New-York-City-meets-Charleston power suit: a hot pink blazer with matching shorts that bared her legs and a blush-colored blouse with an enormous bow tied with a flourish at her throat. On her feet were black ankle boots. No doubt she thought this look let her stand out while fitting in. If so, she'd missed the mark.

"I'm not sure what you're referring to," he replied, returning his attention to his computer monitor.

"You've been offered the CEO position at Gates Multimedia."

He noted she hadn't bragged about where the information had come from, but just knowing it was a subtle reminder that she'd outsmarted him.

"I have."

Instead of taking a seat in one of his guest chairs, she settled her palms on his desk and leaned forward. "They must be very excited to have someone of your caliber taking over."

Was Teagan playing games? Hadn't she spoken to Sienna? Ethan struggled to keep the surprise off his face as he processed this. Did Teagan not yet realize her entire scheme had blown up in her face or was she unaware that he'd turned down his mother's offer? There was only one way to find out.

"I turned them down."

Teagan's eyelashes flickered as she absorbed his declaration, the only sign that she was stunned by his news. Whoever coined the phrase, "Never let them see you sweat," must've taken a page from Teagan Burns's playbook.

"But why? I would think you'd jump at the chance to run your family's multimillion-dollar corporation." As she would surely jump at the chance to run Watts Shipping once he was out of the way.

"Except my place is here." He paused for a beat, letting his stare crystallize into something hard and cutting, before adding, "At *my* family's multimillion-dollar corporation."

Only the most subtle tightening of her lips betrayed that she was annoyed at the emphasis he'd put on *my*.

"But surely you won't be taking over here for many,

many years whereas you could step right into the top position at Gates Multimedia."

She straightened, showing less confidence than she had when she'd first arrived.

"Yes, but Watts Shipping is where I belong."

"Of course," Teagan soothed, "but I'll bet your real mother would love it if you joined your birth family's company instead. After all, if she hadn't given you up, all this time you would've been her obvious successor."

"She didn't give me up," he explained, unsure why it was important for her to know that he'd been wanted all along. "My grandfather thought seventeen was too young for her to be a mother and arranged to have me adopted. She thought I'd died."

"Oh, that's terrible. She must've been devastated to lose you."

For the first time since he'd met her, Ethan heard something in Teagan's voice that resonated with him. They'd both been adopted as infants. And in both cases their mothers hadn't given them up. Teagan's mother had died. Ethan's had been tricked. Until he'd heard the true story about what happened to him, he hadn't understood how much pain he'd been in at the thought of being abandoned by the woman who'd given birth to him.

Suddenly, Ethan was weary of all the verbal fencing. "Cut the crap."

"I'm sorry?" She blinked at him in poorly feigned confusion.

"I know what you've been up to…" Ethan cued up

the first anonymous email he'd been sent and showed it to her. "...all along."

Teagan read the message and stiffened in surprise. A second later she glanced at him, a small smile playing on her lips.

"Someone you don't know sends you an inflammatory email lying about me and you take it as a fact?" She paused to let her dismissive tone sink in. "Is that how you plan to operate Watts Shipping if you're chosen to lead this business? You're going to chase rumors and lies? If that's true then maybe you're not the person who should be in charge."

Ethan had paid careful attention to her reaction and suspected she knew who was behind the message. Although she tried to mask her thoughts, she was obviously shaken. Time to capitalize on this moment of weakness.

"Are you denying that you came to Charleston intending to take over Watts Shipping?"

"Are you criticizing me for thinking I deserve a shot at running my family's company?" she responded, acting surprised and offended.

He wasn't fooled by her innocent act. "Deserve a shot..." he murmured ironically. "More like staging a coup."

"Are you seriously afraid of a little competition?" A taunting smile played over her lips.

"Not if it's fair and aboveboard."

"What else could it be?"

"You convincing Sienna to distract me while you

schemed to undermine my position here was hardly honest."

"It didn't take any convincing." Teagan arched her eyebrows. "So, you've known all along what I was up to and turned my sister's attraction to you to your own advantage. Well played."

Teagan's calculated assessment recalled the argument between him and Sienna. She'd seemed genuinely distraught at being caught participating in her sister's scheme. Not coolly disappointed to be bested as Teagan was at the moment, but cognizant of the repercussions for him.

"Played," he repeated, keeping a firm grip on his fury. "So, you admit you've been treating this as a big game."

"Don't use my words against me. I saw an opportunity and I took it. There's nothing wrong with that."

"You twisted your sister's emotions for your own ends. In my book that's not what family members do to each other."

"She likes you. I thought you liked her. It seemed as if she could use a little fun. That's all I was thinking about."

For an instant he recalled Sienna's face as she realized that he'd slept with her after finding out that she'd been blackballed from the primary art market for her sketchy activities. No doubt she'd felt betrayed. Well, that was nothing compared to how he'd felt as he'd stood before his parents yesterday.

"Well, just so you know, you will never be the CEO of this company." As much satisfaction as he took saying those words, the sense that he had made the right choice was more important.

"That's not really up to you to decide," Teagan countered.

"You're right. It's up to the current chairman of the board—my grandfather—and the current CEO and president—my father. And after I shared with them that you deliberately spilled the story about my trip to Savannah when Sienna asked you not to—"

He actually hadn't said anything, but Teagan wasn't the only one who could use lies and misinformation to throw his opponent off track.

"Did Sienna tell you that?" Teagan interrupted, rolling her eyes. "Of course you believe her."

"She didn't tell me anything. I overheard her asking you to keep quiet yesterday morning."

He paused and waited as her poker face slipped before continuing. "You had no qualms about hurting me or my family to get what you wanted and when they heard that, they were pretty clear that you're not the sort of person they want running the company they spent their lives building."

He watched the lie sink in for several seconds, feeling no guilt whatsoever at the horror and grief she displayed.

She rallied faster than he could've believed possible. "I'm surprised that you went to them with no proof."

"Do you seriously think I need to prove anything to them?" Ethan offered a flat smile. "They know me. They trust me." And then, because he knew from his conversations with Sienna exactly how to push Teagan's buttons, he added, "And I'm not the outsider in this little scenario. You are. I might not be a Watts by blood, but I am family."

The point being that she couldn't come in with her New York City tricks and expect to shatter a lifetime of love. Love. As if the woman had any clue what the word meant. She certainly hadn't shown that she cared for her sister. If she had, she would've known that what she was doing to Sienna would rip her apart.

Sienna was on her way to the front hall with the first of her suitcases when she met her sister storming up the stairs in her direction. Seeing the angry flush coloring Teagan's cheeks, Sienna braced for another confrontation.

"Hey," she began as they met on the landing between the first and second floors. "How come you're home?"

"Declan Scott is the devil!" Teagan declared, her eyes narrowed with murderous intent.

"Well, yes," Sienna agreed, thinking about how many times since they'd first met in high school that Teagan had clashed with the handsome real estate tycoon. "So?"

"So?" Teagan echoed in outrage.

"He's back in New York," Sienna reminded her sister, resisting the urge to roll her eyes at Teagan's melodrama.

"No. He's here. In Charleston. I just ran into him. I don't know when exactly he showed up, but I suspect not long after we arrived."

"What is he doing here?" Sienna clutched the handle of her suitcase to her suddenly churning stomach. When Teagan and Declan were in the same space, their battles had a tendency to damage everyone around them.

Over the years the two strong personalities had struck at each other in a private war that began when Teagan had gone after his sister, who'd been a classmate of Sienna's. She'd never understood what had motivated Teagan, but the incident had caused Declan to notice her and they'd been enemies ever since.

"Ruining everything." Teagan flipped her long hair, eyes becoming arctic jade as she continued, "He tipped Ethan off from the start."

"From the start?" Sienna grabbed for the railing as her knees wobbled. Ethan had known all along that Teagan was out to steal the CEO position from him? "What do you mean? Tipped him off how?"

"He sent Ethan an anonymous email the day we arrived, warning him that I intended on taking over Watts Shipping. He's been playing with me this whole time."

Click. The pieces snapped into place. Was Declan responsible for Ethan learning about her troubles with the New York City galleries? She thought of Ethan's pursuit of her and cringed. The charm that had swept Sienna off her feet took on a sinister quality now that she recognized the manipulation behind it. Every time he'd taken her into his arms, it had been a sham. Every smile he'd bestowed on her. All of it had been a lie. Sienna flushed hot with shame. A second later she shivered as humiliation and despair moved through her like a biting wind off the ocean.

"Why would he do that?" Sienna asked, her fury blazing to life. Declan Scott was one area where the Burns sisters agreed.

"Because it's Declan," Teagan said, tossing her head. "He takes any opportunity to ruin my life."

"And mine, as well," Sienna muttered, recalling all the times the war between the two had spilled over. "Was he the one who told you about why Ethan went to Savannah?"

"No."

Despite Teagan's closed expression, Sienna believed Declan wasn't the source of that information. But her short-term relief ended with her sister's next words.

"Don't worry. I have a plan to get rid of him."

This only reaffirmed Sienna's decision to leave Charleston. "Good luck with that."

As she began moving past her sister, Teagan blocked Sienna's path.

"You can't leave me here alone. Ethan told his entire family that I'm only here to take over the family company."

Good! Yet Sienna couldn't crow about her sister's scheme falling apart. The setback would only cause Teagan to dig in and try harder.

"Isn't it better for you to be up front about your intentions?"

"Are you kidding? Thanks to him they're all going to hate me."

"I'm sure that's not true," Sienna soothed. "But there

is an alternative. You could return to New York and give up this crazy idea of running Watts Shipping." The instant that suggestion left her lips, Sienna realized she'd made a mistake.

"Give up?" Teagan looked appalled. "And let Ethan and Declan win?"

"Win?" Sienna couldn't believe what she was hearing. "This isn't a game. These are real people with real feelings."

"You don't understand. You never have."

"I do understand. Better than you realize. All my life I've been in your shadow. I watched you fight and scheme to be on top. So that everyone would love you." Sienna gulped in air and rushed on. "Why don't you stop relying on your beauty and success and let people love you for who you are?"

Speaking her mind for the first time left her heart pounding so hard she thought she might stroke out. No matter how many times Teagan had hurt her in the past, Sienna loved her and only wished for her to be happy. It just seemed that Teagan was always going about it the wrong way.

"Really?" Teagan sneered. "What would you know about being loved? Our parents adopted me because you weren't good enough."

Compared to what she'd been through with Ethan, this declaration landed like the punch of a downy feather. Sienna's mind went oddly calm. Her relationship with Teagan had always been a complex scramble of love and pain and understanding and exasperation.

"You don't think I know that?" Sienna began.

"Mother placed more value on appearance than anyone I know except perhaps you. I'm not beautiful. And I don't share your aggressive ambition to rule everyone and everything in my orbit. But I am smart and loyal. I have a career I love and friends I trust who support me. Those things might not be important to you, but they matter to me." Rehearsed hundreds of times in her mind, the words poured out of her in a jagged rush. "And the best part of all is that I can look myself in the mirror every day and not be ashamed of who I hurt or the harm I've caused. Can you say the same?"

Sienna was gasping for breath by the time she finished her impassioned speech. Yet in the aftermath of the fervent soliloquy, she wasn't suffused with triumph or vindicated. One look at Teagan's scornful expression left Sienna hollow and empty.

"I don't need you," Teagan declared, her voice low and biting as she headed toward the door. "I never have and I never will."

Fighting tears of helpless frustration, Sienna resumed manhandling her heavy luggage down the endless flights of stairs. She was hot, angry and miserable by the time she exited the house with the second suitcase only to discover that the car pulling into the driveway wasn't her ride to the airport, but was driven by the last person she wanted to see.

"You're leaving?" Ethan asked unnecessarily, eyeing her suitcases.

What did he expect? Even if things between them hadn't exploded into a million shards of anger, resentment and pain, she'd planned to head back to New York in a day or two. Neither one of them had spoken about her staying longer or him visiting her between business trips. The revelations over the last twenty-four hours didn't change the reality that they'd had a fling and now it was over.

"There's an auction in Salzburg coming up next week." She would be bidding on pieces for four clients. "I need to head back to New York to prepare."

"I thought you'd planned to stay a little longer."

"That was before."

Had he already forgotten his brutal indictment of her as Teagan's feckless pawn in the battle for control of Watts Shipping? He couldn't possibly expect that she'd stick around for more abuse?

"And you weren't going to say goodbye?"

Sienna gaped at him. "I thought we already had."

The ride she'd been waiting for pulled into the front driveway and came to a stop behind Ethan's car. She began rolling her luggage toward it as the driver got out and went toward the trunk.

"I spoke with my parents," Ethan began from behind her, his deep voice heavy with anguish and rage. "They are devastated."

She winced as her heart clenched. The impulse to comfort him rose in her, but she gritted her teeth and resisted. He wasn't interested in being consoled by her. He wanted to punish. Handing off her suitcases to the driver, Sienna turned to Ethan.

"Do you feel at all guilty about what you and your sister have done?" he continued, speaking each word with deliberate care, letting his distaste show.

"The only thing I did was not tell you that Teagan wanted to be the next CEO of Watts Shipping," Sienna reiterated, wishing he'd just let her leave. "Besides that, I haven't done anything to you or your family."

"No regrets then?"

"Just one. I regret coming here." Because if she hadn't, she never would've met Ethan or had her heart torn apart in the battle between him and her sister. Sienna sighed. "No, that's not true. I'm glad I met you. I just wish that you weren't like Teagan." Misery shredded her voice. "You knew all along what she was up to and used me to get to her."

She hadn't realized how much it would hurt to face him, knowing that he'd been misleading her about his feelings this whole time. He'd accused her of sleeping with him as part of a scheme, but obviously that was what had motivated his actions. He'd lied to her. Used her desire against her. And he'd manipulated her as if she was nothing but a pawn in his chess match with her sister.

She searched Ethan's expression for remorse or grief, but saw only righteous obstinacy. How had she missed such devious calculation on Ethan's part?

"Stop playing the wronged innocent," he retorted, his tone roughening with irritation. "You could've warned me what Teagan was up to, but you didn't."

"You're right, but to be fair, she's my sister and you're—"

"Just some guy you had sex with?"

"Sure…that." She held strong against the bitterness in his voice and met his eyes without flinching. Maybe she'd been a fool to fall for him in the first place, but she didn't have to keep making the same mistake. "So tell me, if you haven't trusted me from the start, why did you bring me with you to Savannah to meet your family?"

Why make her feel like her company mattered to him? That he appreciated her support and craved her affection?

"Maybe because I was curious to see how far you would go for her." He leaned toward her, pinning her with his dark stare. "I guess this weekend I found out."

Sienna recoiled from the implication that she'd seduced him to gain his trust. "I didn't sleep with you to help my sister."

"No?"

"No. I care about you and I thought you felt the same way about me." Sienna put her hand on his forearm. When his forbidding expression remained unchanged, she let it fall back to her side. "Until today I had no idea how wrong I was."

"I had to know what you were up to."

How had she been so blind? She should've recognized that it was beyond crazy that Ethan could be falling for her.

Sienna offered him a tight smile. "I guess that means we can both stop pretending that last weekend meant something."

"It meant something to me," he said in a shocking turnaround, his expression like granite, his gaze steady and sincere.

"Damn you, Ethan Watts," she cried, confused and

terrified by the way her heart reached for him. "I'm done being manipulated by you. Now, if you'll kindly move." Desperation gave her the strength to wedge her laptop case into the space between him and the car and shift him aside. "I have a plane to catch. And I really can't afford to miss it."

Thirteen

The two days following Sienna's departure from Charleston didn't go as Ethan expected they would. He assumed that with her gone and Teagan rethinking her strategy, his emotions would calm and his focus would shift back to work, socializing and family time. Instead, he caught himself snapping at his employees, brooding alone at his house and turning down invitations from everyone. In fact, his antisocial behavior had gotten so bad that he'd stopped answering calls altogether.

Which was why he wasn't all that surprised when Paul appeared in his office with no warning, a thick file in his hand. "So, I finally got a line on your anonymous friend," his brother said, skipping the lecture about how the family was worried about him.

Ethan stuck out his hand and accepted the file. "I thought you said the email address was impossible to track."

"Did I say that?" Paul smirked. "Maybe what I should've said was that it was impossible to track through normal channels."

"Do I want to ask?" Ethan began, knowing when his brother started talking about the dark web it was like watching a foreign language film without subtitles. "Nope, I don't wanna know. Who is he or she?"

Paul slouched in one of Ethan's guest chairs and propped his cheek on his hand. "A guy by the name of Declan Scott."

Ethan scanned the file without registering much of the data. His thoughts churned as he imagined what he'd like to do to the guy whose misinformation had made Ethan doubt Sienna.

"Aside from the fact that he's from New York, how is he connected to Teagan?" he asked.

"They attended the same high school, although they were three years apart. Since then they've appeared at the same events, but never together. They have friends in common, but from what I can gather they can't stand each other."

Having been on the receiving end of Teagan's scheming, it made sense that she would've made enemies. "Okay, so that explains why the guy warned me against her, but what's with all the cloak-and-dagger business?" Ethan spread several photos across his desk, of Declan Scott. He looked like an aloof Ralph Lauren model, with classic *Town & Country* stuffiness. "But what does he get out of involving himself in our business here in Charleston?"

"Why don't you ask him?" Paul got to his feet. "He has a suite at Hotel Bennett."

"He's here?" The news propelled Ethan to his feet. He snatched up his car keys. It was the most alive he'd felt in two days. "I don't suppose you got a room number."

Ten minutes later Ethan was heading for the boutique hotel. He had attended several parties there, including one wedding, and been to Gabrielle, their signature restaurant, on several occasions. In fact, if he and Sienna hadn't gone to Savannah, he would've taken her there.

He'd lost count of the number of times over the last two days when he'd imaged how Sienna would've reacted to a place or an experience. Thoughts of her consumed him. As did the melancholy he couldn't seem to shake since she'd left. And as many times as he'd reminded himself what she'd done and that he couldn't possibly care about someone who'd been working against him, nothing seemed to ease the constant ache in his chest.

He missed her. All the damned time. No matter how angry he was with her for what she'd done. No matter how many times he called himself a stubborn fool for allowing himself to trust her with his secrets and fears. Despite all that had happened, Ethan couldn't shake the certainty that he'd been wrong to let her go back to New York.

The lack of closure was making him crazy. That

was the only thing that could account for his sleepless nights and manic restlessness.

At the hotel, Ethan pounded on the door to Declan Scott's suite, letting his frustration out. The man who answered was tall, lean and dressed in a crisp navy suit, but not Declan Scott.

"I'm here to speak to your boss," Ethan said, comfortable with his assumption that the busy real estate mogul wouldn't stop working even while away from New York.

"He's—"

"Let him in," a voice called from inside the suite, the laconic tones rich with amusement.

Ethan found his quarry idling on the sofa, a tumbler of amber liquid dangling from his long fingers. The New Yorker made no move to rise and greet his guest, prompting Ethan to set aside his southern politeness and charm.

"So you're my anonymous friend?" Ethan twisted the last word into an insult as he surveyed the tall man. "Declan Scott, is it?"

The other man inclined his head. "Sorry we're meeting under such difficult circumstances."

"Difficult circumstances?" Ethan fumed at Scott's utter lack of sincerity. He so obviously didn't give a damn that his meddling had ripped apart Ethan's world. "You caused this mess."

"I didn't." Scott's calm fanned Ethan's temper, making it flare even hotter. "All I did was warn you about Teagan. You chose how to use the information."

Was this the sort of reckless game they played in

New York? If that was the case then maybe he was glad that Sienna was gone.

A dagger-thrust of pain in his chest said otherwise.

"What exactly was your purpose in contacting me?" Ethan demanded, making no attempt to disguise his disgust.

"I didn't think you were up to the challenge of dealing with Teagan on your own. She can be quite a handful." Scott assessed him with a pointed look. "Was I wrong?"

Ethan ignored the question. "So what's your interest in all of this?"

"Teagan refuses to let me have something I want." Scott tugged at his shirt cuff. "I decided to show her how that feels."

Whoa. Ethan mentally reviewed the additional information Paul had uncovered about Teagan and her connection to Declan Scott. The pair had been sworn enemies since the beginning. Although the reason why escaped him. Had they rubbed each other wrong from the start? Had they once been close and had a falling out? Or had they loved each other at first sight?

Ethan recalled his own reaction when he'd glimpsed Sienna on the driveway outside his grandfather's home. And the hurt in her eyes the day she left. Pain he'd caused.

Rather than face his guilt, Ethan attacked the man before him. "But it wasn't just Teagan you harmed with your games."

"My games?" Lazy amusement curved Scott's lips.

"You're one to talk You've been playing games of your own with Sienna."

The accusation hit home, but Ethan countered hotly, "You fed me misleading information."

"Seems to me," Scott began, his level of detachment impossibly high, "that you are blaming me for your failure to trust the woman you love."

Love.

"I don't know what you're talking about. I'm not in love."

What did Ethan know about that emotion? He knew how he felt about the parents who'd raised him and the grandfather who believed in him. He would do anything for the Shaw twins and his brother, Paul. Yet he'd been holding back his heart for a long time. Not believing they could possibly love him because he wasn't one of them, he'd gone through the motions of being a good son, brother, friend and ally. He'd spread his charm around, but hadn't truly given of himself.

With Sienna it had been different.

He'd opened up to her about his feelings of isolation and let her glimpse his fear of not being loved. She in turn shared what it was like to grow up feeling unworthy and unloved. He felt closer to her than anyone he'd ever known. So, of course, he'd messed it up.

Unable to believe that her friendship and affection had come without strings, he'd asked her to choose him over her sister. She'd refused and he'd used that as proof that she was against him. He hadn't trusted that her feelings for him could possibly be real. The sting of betrayal had been a loud screech in his brain, drowning out all rational thought.

"So you're perfectly fine since Sienna returned to New York?"

"How did you—?"

Ethan never finished the question. It didn't matter how Declan knew so much. What consumed him was Sienna's absence. He was definitely not fine. Being without her these last few days was proof that the joy she'd brought into his life was addictive and made everything brighter and clear.

"You don't wish things had turned out differently?" Declan Scott continued. "Like perhaps if you'd given her the benefit of the doubt that you might still be together?"

The way the man asked the question—as if he already knew the answer—irritated Ethan. The level of the New Yorker's insight into Ethan's private thoughts spooked him. It was almost as if Scott had an inside track to the hell Ethan had been going through. A hell the other man had been partially responsible for creating with his misleading emails about Sienna.

"Look," Ethan said, realizing that his initial reason for confronting Scott no longer mattered. Sienna had been the victim in the feud between her sister and this man. Criticizing her for being loyal to her sister hadn't been fair. "I don't give a damn what sort of twisted games you and Teagan play, but going forward, leave Sienna alone."

"Or?"

"You'll find out, if you ever bother Sienna again."

Without waiting for Scott's comeback, Ethan turned and strode from the suite.

The confrontation with Scott had given Ethan's perceptions a much-needed reset. Before leaving Charleston, Sienna had confessed to caring for him, but he'd been too angry and stubborn to believe her. Now, with the New Yorker's words compelling Ethan to confront his feelings for Sienna, memories of their time together ran on a loop in his brain. Too late, he was grasping that the reason he'd been so drawn to her was that they both felt like outsiders around the people they loved. Yet with her, he'd known a sense of belonging that made everything better.

And instead of sharing his heart with her, he'd let her board a plane and fly away.

Could he fix it? Would she give him the chance? One thing was certain: he couldn't win her heart from here in Charleston. He needed a boots-on-the-ground approach and that meant flying to New York City.

And if in his absence Teagan got the toehold she was after at Watts Shipping?

Ethan brushed aside the question. No career was more important than being with the woman of his dreams.

Following the art auction in Salzburg, Sienna took a few extra days in Europe to reach out to some of her contacts and pursue leads on new clients. Throwing herself into work offered a temporary reprieve from heartache, but she couldn't run herself ragged indefinitely and after ten days, she returned to New York.

While the plane taxied to the terminal, Sienna checked her messages and spotted a text from Gia. Worn out by endless, sleepless nights trying not to think about Ethan[, Sienna had neglected to organize a car to pick her up. To her delight, Gia had taken matters into her own hands and a driver would be waiting in the baggage claim area to drive her into Manhattan.

But when Sienna stepped off the escalator, the man holding a sign with her name on it was the last person she expected to see. With her heart in her throat and her mind struggling to adjust to seeing Ethan in New York, she shuffled toward him.

"What are you doing here?" she demanded, wishing she wasn't quite so overjoyed.

"I came to see you."

How dare he spring this surprise visit on her and embroil her friend in the scheme. Sienna would have to have a stern chat with Gia. "I really wish you hadn't."

"I don't believe you mean that."

"Believe it." With a rude snort, she turned her back on him and marched toward the carousel, hoping to spot her luggage and get the hell away from Ethan. She wasn't surprised when he followed her.

"I'm sorry how I handled things with you about the whole Teagan-wanting-to-be-CEO thing."

She shot him a sidelong glance. "Neither one of us deserves stellar marks for what we did."

"I shouldn't have gotten angry because you wanted to help your sister."

Sienna held firm against her longing to have everything be all right between them. He'd hurt her and she wasn't going to let a few pretty words lead her astray again.

Conscious that they were in a crowded airport, she lowered her voice. "But you do realize that I didn't help her by sleeping with you to get information?"

"Yes." He dropped his volume to match hers. "Deep down I knew better than to believe something like that."

A familiar piece of luggage was gliding in their direction and Sienna began moving to intercept it. Ethan was there before her, his strong arm reaching past her to snag the handle and lift it off the silver belt as if it weighed significantly less than its forty-six pounds. If she'd hoped to secure her suitcase and escape Ethan in a taxi, she was doomed to be frustrated. Instead, she ended up chasing after him as he moved purposefully toward the exit that would take them to the helicopter shuttle leaving for Manhattan.

Sienna withdrew into herself and maintained radio silence as they switched from shuttle to helicopter to taxi. She grappled with the conflict between her instincts and her brain. One wanted to believe that everything would be okay now that he recognized he'd been wrong. The other insisted that misunderstanding hadn't created the problems between them, but Ethan's lack of trust and her failure to be up-front with him had.

When it became obvious outside her building that she wasn't going to shake Ethan until they cleared the air, Sienna invited him up. As the elevator ascended, she turned to face him.

"Look, if you want to be friendly because my sister is your cousin, then I can do that." She noticed his whole manner brighten and didn't know what to make of it. "But really, this could've been resolved over the phone. You didn't have to come all the way to New York."

"But if I called, you might've avoided answering and I wanted to make sure you knew just how serious I am about making things right between us."

While she wasn't immune to his enticing half smile and earnest puppy-dog eyes, her weeks apart from him had sharpened her need for self-preservation.

Making herself sound as prickly and forbidding as possible, she said, "We could've video chatted."

"We could've," he murmured, his voice whiskey smooth. "But don't they say make-up sex is the best?"

Sienna would give anything to stop the way her body electrified at the thought of being in his arms once more. Heat flooded her cheeks despite her best effort to remain aloof and immune. She shoved her hands into her pockets to avoid snatching his lapels and yanking him toward her. As much as she wanted to give in to her longing, she didn't know if she was strong enough to have sex with him one last time, and then say goodbye.

"I think what happened in Savannah should stay in Savannah, don't you?"

This didn't crush him the way she hoped. Fortunately, the elevator doors opened and she was able to make a break for it. Once again, she realized escaping Ethan was impossible.

"Not at all." His long stride eliminated her brief

lead, and he matched her pace as they drew near her apartment door. "I refuse to believe that we're done."

Pausing outside her apartment, she gaped at him. After they'd spent their time together lying to each other about what was going on with Teagan and the CEO position at Watts Shipping, how could he possibly think they had any chance in hell of making something work? Yet her skin prickled as joy rushed through her. Did he want to put the past behind them and start fresh?

No. Impossible.

"Done?" She drew in a shaky breath before continuing. "I don't think we ever got started."

"I disagree."

"You were so busy suspecting me of conspiring against you that we never had a chance to develop real feelings for each other." She paused and smiled through her pain. "Besides, from the moment we met, I knew that it was only a matter of time before you'd move onto someone new."

"So, I was just a fling for you?"

Was that actual disappointment in his dark brown eyes? Sienna badly wanted to believe that she'd meant something to him.

"It started that way," she admitted, biting her lip to keep from confessing more. "Whatever. Look, none of this matters now."

"It matters to me."

"Why?" She wished he'd stop tormenting her with possibilities. "Can you honestly say that after what happened we can put the past behind us?"

"I can and I will." Ethan took her hands in his and

squeezed until she met his gaze. "Asking you to come with me to meet my family had nothing to do with your sister or her schemes. I wanted you with me. I didn't understand at the time why I valued your companionship and your support, but now I do."

Although Sienna dropped her gaze from his beguiling expression, she was already too susceptible to hope. Could she trust that he'd had a change of heart?

"I've had a lot of time to put things in perspective these last few weeks," Sienna began, tears stinging her eyes as she forced herself to be rational. "What stands out to me is that you and Teagan both want everyone to admire you. It's all showmanship and sparkle. And I fall for it every time."

"You fell for me?" A wicked smile kicked up one corner of his lips.

"This isn't a good thing." Sienna scowled at him, edging ever closer to despair. "I realize that I have a type and that type is charming and manipulative."

Tears blurred her vision as she shoved her key into the lock. She got it in on the first try, stunned that her shaking hands hadn't made this impossible. Twisting the doorknob, she then threw the door open.

"But you did fall." When she refused to repeat her confession, he seized her by the shoulders and gave her a little shake. "I fell for you, as well."

"I'm over it now." She broke free of his grip and shoved her suitcase ahead of her into the apartment.

"Well, I'm not," Ethan called after her. "I fell hard. Harder than I imagined possible."

Five half-stumbling steps later, she burst into the

living room and gaped at the extravagant bouquets that filled the space with scent and color. Multiple surfaces held gigantic flower arrangements but the centerpiece was a massive display of red roses.

"I love you, Sienna."

She whipped around and spotted him standing four feet away. Everything seemed to freeze. Her heart. Her lungs. Ethan's earnest expression. It was as if his words had hit the pause button on her life, allowing her thoughts and feelings to process every moment they'd spent together and make sense of the rush of data.

"You love me?" she repeated, experimenting with the words. "You can't."

"I can and I do." His teeth flashed, amusement brightening his whole appearance. He came toward her with his hands outstretched, but even though her whole body ached for his embrace, she backed away.

"But how? I mean, after everything with Teagan... You hate me." This last came out as a ragged whisper.

"Never." He seized her hands and raised them to his lips. "I was angry and scared, but never, ever did I hate you." Ethan wrapped one arm around her waist and brought her tight against him. "For a long time I felt like I was on the outside looking in. And then you came along and that feeling stopped. Being with you makes me feel like I'm a part of something. The whole thing about being adopted wasn't what was eating at me. It was that I'd closed myself off to everyone I loved. You changed that."

"I love you," Sienna blurted out, the words exploding from her in a gush of relief. "I thought I was crazy to feel such a strong connection to you so fast, but every moment with you makes me so happy."

"And I want you to continue to feel that way. Whatever it takes. If it means I give up Watts Shipping so there's peace between us and Teagan…"

"I can't ask you to do that for me." While Sienna appreciated that he was ready to make sacrifices for her, their relationship would only work if both of them were happy. "You asked me to side with you against Teagan and I'm willing to do that. You are my family now. My loyalty is yours no matter what."

Sienna wrapped her arms around Ethan's neck and brought her lips into contact with his. The kiss held both passion and promise. Loving him made her world better and she was beyond blissful that they'd found a way past their mistakes.

"You're the most fascinating and genuine woman I know," Ethan said, his eyes soft with affection and joy. "I love that you're brilliant and funny, not to mention obsessed with learning interesting facts about everywhere you go. You knew exactly what to say when I grappled with finding my birth mother and how to give me the space to process my feelings. Your curves go on for days and sex with you is the best I've ever had." He grew serious. "I've never been comfortable being myself around anyone the way I can be with you. It's peaceful and feels like home."

"That's how I feel when I'm with you."

"Then I hope that means you see us having a future."

"Of course. In fact, I'd already given some thought to moving to Charleston."

"You don't say," he teased, dropping a kiss on her nose. "Well, I'm glad to hear that, because I want to marry you, Sienna Burns."

Sienna smiled as she realized the future she'd dreamed about while in Savannah with Ethan was about to become a reality. "I love you and want to spend the rest of my life with you as Mrs. Ethan Watts."

They sealed the moment with a long, hungry kiss that left them out of breath and grinning.

"Now, I'll be wanting to put this on your finger." Ethan produced a gorgeous solitaire diamond ring. "So you can't take back your promise to be with me always."

As stunning as the ring was, Sienna only had eyes for the man who slid it over her knuckle and into place on her left hand. "Always and forever."

* * * * *

If you loved Sienna and Ethan,
You won't want to miss
Teagan's story,
coming soon
from Cat Schield
and available exclusively
from Harlequin Desire!

#2809 TEXAS TOUGH
Texas Cattleman's Club: Heir Apparent • by Janice Maynard
World-traveling documentary filmmaker Abby Carmichael is only in Royal
for a short project, definitely not to fall for hometown rancher Carter Crane.
But opposites attract and the sparks between them ignite! Can they look
past their differences for something more than temporary?

#2810 ONE WEEK TO CLAIM IT ALL
Sambrano Studios • by Adriana Herrera
The illegitimate daughter of a telenovela mogul, Esmeralda Sambrano
is shocked to learn *she's* the successor to his empire, much to the
chagrin of her father's protégé, Rodrigo Almanzar. Tension soon turns to
passion, but will a common enemy ruin everything?

#2811 FAKE ENGAGEMENT, NASHVILLE STYLE
Dynasties: Beaumont Bay • by Jules Bennett
Tired of being Nashville's most eligible bachelor, Luke Sutherland
needs a fake date to the wedding of the year, and his ex lover,
Cassandra Taylor, needs a favor. But as they masquerade as a couple,
one hot kiss makes things all too real...

#2812 A NINE-MONTH TEMPTATION
Brooklyn Nights • by Joanne Rock
Sable Cordero's dream job as a celebrity stylist is upended after she
spends one sexy night with fashion CEO Roman Zayn. When he learns
Sable is pregnant, he promises to take care of his child, nothing more.
But neither anticipated the attraction still between them...

#2813 WHAT HAPPENS IN MIAMI...
Miami Famous • by Nadine Gonzalez
Actor Alessandro Cardenas isn't just attending Miami's hottest art event
for the parties. He's looking to find who forged his grandfather's famous
paintings. When he meets gallerist Angeline Louis, he can't resist at
least one night...but will that lead to betrayal?

#2814 CORNER OFFICE SECRETS
Men of Maddox Hill • by Shannon McKenna
Chief finance officer Vann Acosta is not one to mix business with
pleasure—until he meets stunning cybersecurity expert Sophie Valente.
Their chemistry is undeniable, but when she uncovers the truth, will
company secrets change everything?

Get 4 FREE REWARDS!

We'll send you 2 FREE Books plus 2 FREE Mystery Gifts.

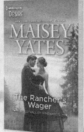

Harlequin Desire books transport you to the world of the American elite with juicy plot twists, delicious sensuality and intriguing scandal.

FREE Value Over $20

YES! Please send me 2 FREE Harlequin Desire novels and my 2 FREE gifts (gifts are worth about $10 retail). After receiving them, if I don't wish to receive any more books, I can return the shipping statement marked "cancel." If I don't cancel, I will receive 6 brand-new novels every month and be billed just $4.55 per book in the U.S. or $5.24 per book in Canada. That's a savings of at least 13% off the cover price! It's quite a bargain! Shipping and handling is just 50¢ per book in the U.S. and $1.25 per book in Canada.* I understand that accepting the 2 free books and gifts places me under no obligation to buy anything. I can always return a shipment and cancel at any time. The free books and gifts are mine to keep no matter what I decide.

225/326 HDN GNND

Name (please print)

Address   Apt. #

City   State/Province   Zip/Postal Code

Email: Please check this box ☐ if you would like to receive newsletters and promotional emails from Harlequin Enterprises ULC and its affiliates. You can unsubscribe anytime.

Mail to the Harlequin Reader Service:
IN U.S.A.: P.O. Box 1341, Buffalo, NY 14240-8531
IN CANADA: P.O. Box 603, Fort Erie, Ontario L2A 5X3

Want to try 2 free books from another series! Call 1-800-873-8635 or visit www.ReaderService.com.

---

*Terms and prices subject to change without notice. Prices do not include sales taxes, which will be charged (if applicable) based on your state or country of residence. Canadian residents will be charged applicable taxes. Offer not valid in Quebec. This offer is limited to one order per household. Books received may not be as shown. Not valid for current subscribers to Harlequin Desire books. All orders subject to approval. Credit or debit balances in a customer's account(s) may be offset by any other outstanding balance owed by or to the customer. Please allow 4 to 6 weeks for delivery. Offer available while quantities last.

Your Privacy—Your information is being collected by Harlequin Enterprises ULC, operating as Harlequin Reader Service. For a complete summary of the information we collect, how we use this information and to whom it is disclosed, please visit our privacy notice located at corporate.harlequin.com/privacy-notice. From time to time we may also exchange your personal information with reputable third parties. If you wish to opt out of this sharing of your personal information, please visit readerservice.com/consumerschoice or call 1-800-873-8635. **Notice to California Residents**—Under California law, you have specific rights to control and access your data. For more information on these rights and how to exercise them, visit corporate.harlequin.com/california-privacy.

HD21R

Love Harlequin romance?

DISCOVER.

Be the first to find out about promotions, news and exclusive content!

Facebook.com/HarlequinBooks

Twitter.com/HarlequinBooks

Instagram.com/HarlequinBooks

Pinterest.com/HarlequinBooks

ReaderService.com

EXPLORE.

Sign up for the Harlequin e-newsletter and download a free book from any series at **TryHarlequin.com**

CONNECT.

Join our Harlequin community to share your thoughts and connect with other romance readers!
Facebook.com/groups/HarlequinConnection